HEAVEN AND HELL

JÓN KALMAN STEFÁNSSON

HEAVEN AND HELL

Translated from the Icelandic by
Philip Roughton

MACLEHOSE PRESS
QUERCUS · LONDON

First published in Great Britain in 2010 by MacLehose Press
This paperback edition published in 2011

MacLehose Press
an imprint of Quercus
55 Baker Street
7th Floor, South Block
London W1U 8EW

First published in Iceland as *Himnaríki og helvíti* by Bjartur, Reykjavik, 2008
Copyright © Jón Kalman Stefánsson 2007

English translation copyright © Philip Roughton 2010
Published by agreement with Leonhardt & Høier Literary Agency A/S, Copenhagen

This book has been published with the financial support
of Bókmenntasjóður/The Icelandic Literature Fund

Bókmenntasjóður
The Icelandic Literature Fund

The moral right of Jón Kalman Stefánsson to be
identified as the author of this work has been
asserted in accordance with the Copyright,
Designs and Patents Act, 1988.

A CIP catalogue record for this book is available
from the British Library

ISBN 978 1 84916 406 1

10 9 8 7 6 5 4 3 2 1

Set in Albertina by Libanus Press Ltd
Printed and bound in Great Britain by Clays Ltd, St Ives plc

HEAVEN AND HELL

We Are Nearly Darkness

The mountains tower above life and death and these houses huddling together on the Spit. We live at the bottom of a bowl, the day passes, turns to evening, it is filled with the serenity of darkness and then the stars kindle. They glitter eternally above us as if they have an urgent message, but what message and from whom? What do they want from us, or, perhaps more importantly, what do we want from them?

There is little left of us resembling light. We stand much closer to darkness, are nearly darkness, all that we have left are memories and the hope that has nevertheless faded, continues to fade and soon resembles an extinguished star, a dark chunk of stone. Yet we know a little about life and a little about death, and can tell of it: we come all this way to touch you, and to effect destiny.

We intend to tell of those who lived in our days, more than a hundred years ago, and are little more to you than names on leaning crosses and cracked headstones. Life and memories that were effaced according to the merciless ordinances of time. This we intend to change. Our words are a kind of rescue team on a relentless mission to save past events and extinguished lives from the black hole of oblivion, and that is no easy task; along the way they are welcome to find some answers, then get us out of here before it is too late. Let this suffice for now, we'll send the words on to you, those bewildered, scattered rescue teams unsure of their task, all compasses broken, maps torn or out of date, yet you should welcome them. Then we shall see what happens.

3

The Boy, the Sea
and the Loss of Paradise

I

This was during the years when we were surely still alive. The month of March and the world white with snow, although not purely white, here it is never purely white, no matter how much snow falls, even though sky and sea freeze together and the cold penetrates deep into the heart where dreams have their home, the colour white never wins. The cliff-belts on the mountains rip it off as soon as it falls and jut out, black as coal, into the white world. They jut out black over the boy and Bárður as they walk away from the Village, our origin and end, the centre of the world. The centre of the world is laughable and proud. They walk easily, young legs, fire that burns, but they are also racing against the darkness, which is perhaps fitting since human life is a constant race against the darkness of the world, the treachery, the cruelty, the cowardice, a race that often seems so hopeless, yet we still run and, as we do, hope lives on. Bárður and the boy, however, intend only to overtake the darkness or twilight of the air, beat it to the huts, the fishing huts, walk sometimes side by side, which is by far the best because tracks that lie side by side are a sign of solidarity, then life is not quite so lonely. The path, however, is often not more than a single track that winds like a frozen snake in the snow and then the boy has to look at the backs of Bárður's shoes, at the skin bag he carries on his back, at the black tangled hair and the head that sits securely on the broad shoulders. Sometimes they walk across stony beaches, tread risky paths on cliff faces, it is worst on the Impassable, a cable fastened to the rock face, a sheer mountainside above, a sheer stone wall below and the surging green sea, a thirty-metre fall, the mountainside rises nearly six hundred metres into the air and the peak is covered in clouds. The sea on one side, steep and lofty mountains on the other; therein lies our whole story. The authorities, merchants, might rule our destitute days, but the mountains and the sea rule life, they are our fate, or that's the way we think sometimes, and that's the way you certainly would feel if you had awakened and slept for decades beneath the same mountains, if your chest had risen and fallen with the breath of the sea on our cockleshells. There is hardly anything as beautiful as the sea on good days, or clear nights, when it dreams and the gleam of the moon is its dream. But the sea is not a bit beautiful, and we hate it more than anything else when the waves rise dozens of metres above the boat, when the sea breaks over it and, no matter how much we wave our hands, invoke God and Jesus, it drowns us like wretched whelps. Then all are equal. Rotten bastards and good men, giants and laggards, the happy and the sad. There are shouts, a few frantic gestures, and then it's as if we were never here, the dead body sinks, the blood

8

panting like an old dog but it's as if you haven't taken a single step today. Bárður looks at him with those brown, austral eyes of his and grins. Some of us have brown eyes, fishermen come here from distant places and have done so for hundreds of years because the sea is a treasure chest. They come from France, Spain, many of them with brown eyes, and some leave the colour of their eyes behind with a woman, sail away, return home or drown.

Yes, it's about time, Bárður agrees. It's been half a month since their last fishing voyage. First a storm raged from the south-east, it rained, the ground became spotted and dark where it emerged from the snow, then the wind changed and came from the north, lashing its snowstorm whip for days on end. Storm, rain and snow for fourteen days, not a boat on the sea and the fish safe from humans for the time being, down in the deep stillness of the sea, where storms cannot reach; men seen there are drowned. One can say various things about drowned men but at least they don't catch fish, they actually don't catch anything except the gleam of the moon on the surface. Two weeks and sometimes one couldn't move from one hut to another because of the weather, the howling storm wiped out the entire landscape in all directions, the sky, the horizon, even time itself, long since finished fixing what needed to be fixed, tied on the cod hooks, untangled the line, untangled all snarls except those related to the heart and the sex drive. A man or two struggled along the beaches, searching for mussels for bait, some used the time to make things, mended the waterproofs, but days spent tied to the shore can be long, they can stretch into endlessness. It's easiest to endure the wait with card games, play and play and never stand up except to attend to bodily functions, trudge out into the storm and relieve oneself among rocks on the beach, some, however, so lazy, or perhaps not so beautiful inside, don't bother going down to the beach and instead shit right up near the huts, then say to the Superintendent as they're coming back in, a project for you, pal! The boy is the hut's super and thus has to clean up around it, he is the youngest, the weakest, could beat no-one in a wrestling match, and he was assigned the Superintendent's post, that's how life frequently is, those who aren't strong enough have to clean up others' shit. Two long weeks and when the weather finally settled it looked quite as if the world had returned, look, there's the sky, so it's true, it exists, and the horizon is a fact! Yesterday the storm's fury had slackened so much that they could clear rocks from the landing, clambered down there, twelve in number from both huts, two crews, toiled away moving huge stones tossed by the sea onto the landing, mere pebbles beneath which they lost their footing, scratched and bloodied themselves, six hours of labour on the slippery fore-shore. This morning a wind blew from the west, rather weakly, but when it blows from the west the breakers frequently make voyages impossible, it's a crying shame, almost vilifying, to see this foam-ing obstruction and the sea beyond it more or less calm enough for sailing. One's temper is soothed, however, by knowing that cod shy away in the western wind, simply vanish, and besides, it provides an excellent opportunity to make a trip into town. Men left the main huts in groups, the beaches teeming and the mountainsides crawling with fishermen.

Bárður and the boy sometimes catch a glimpse of the group ahead of them and modify their pace in such a way that they draw farther apart rather than closer together, the two of them travel by themselves, it's best that way, so much that needs to be said intended for just the two of them, about poetry, about dreams and the things that cause us sleepless nights.

They have just crossed over the Impassable. From here it is approximately a half-hour's walk home to the hut, for the most part along the stony beach where the sea snaps at them. They stand high up on the slope, put off the descent, look out over more than ten kilometres of cold blue sea that tosses and turns as if impatient at the head of the fjord, and at the white beach opposite. The snow never fully leaves it, no summer manages to melt the snow completely, and still folk live wherever there is even a trace of a bay. Wherever the sea is fairly accessible there stands a farm, and at midsummer the little home-field surrounding it turns green, pale green areas of tussocky ground stretch up the mountainside and yellow dandelions kindle in the grass, but even further away, to the north-east, they see more mountains rise into the grey winter sky: these are the Strands, where the world ends. Bárður removes his bag, takes out a bottle of *brennivín*, they both take a gulp. Bárður sighs, looks off to the left, looks at the ocean itself, deep and dark, he doesn't think at all about the end of the world and the eternal cold, but instead about long, dark hair, how it blew in her face in early January and how the most precious hand in the world brushed it aside, her name is Sigríður, and Bárður trembles a bit inside when he speaks the name to himself. The boy follows his friend's glance and sighs as well. He wants to accomplish something in life, learn languages, see the world, read a thousand books, he wants to discover the core, whatever that might be, he wants to discover whether there is any core, but sometimes it's hard to think and read when one is stiff and sore after a difficult fishing voyage, wet and cold after twelve hours' working in the meadows, when his thoughts can be so heavy that he can hardly lift them, then it's a long way to the core.

The west wind blows and the sky slowly darkens above their heads

Dammit, the boy blurts out, because he is standing there alone with his thoughts, Bárður has set off down the slope, the wind is blowing, the sea churns and Bárður is thinking about dark hair, about warm laughter, about big eyes bluer than the sky on a clear June night. They have come down to the beach. They clamber over large rocks, the afternoon continues to darken and press in on them, they keep going and hurry the final minutes, and are a hair's breadth ahead of the twilight to the huts.

These are two pairs of new-ish huts with lofts located just above the landing, two sixereens overturned on the beach and lashed down. A large, rough crag extends into the sea just beyond the huts, making landings there easier but overshadowing the main fishing huts, which are a half-hour's walk away, thirty to forty huts and more than half of them fairly new like theirs, with sleeping lofts, but a number of them from a former time and one-storeyed, the crews sleep and bait the lines and eat in the same space. Thirty to forty buildings, perhaps fifty, we don't remember exactly, so much is forgotten, confused: we have also learned little by little to trust the feeling, not the memory.

Dammit, nothing but adverts, mutters Bárður. They have entered the hut, gone up to the loft, sit on the bed, there are four beds for the six men and the Custodian, the woman who takes care of the cooking, the wood-burning stove, the cleaning. Bárður and the boy sleep head-to-toe, I sleep with your toes, the boy says sometimes, all he has to do is turn his head and his friend's woollen socks are in his face. Bárður has big feet, he has pulled his feet up beneath him and murmurs, nothing but adverts, meaning the newspaper published in the Village, which comes weekly, is four pages long, the last page frequently covered with advertisements. Bárður lays the paper aside and they finish removing from their bags everything that makes life worth living if we exclude, in their case, red lips, dreams and soft hair. It's not possible to put red lips and dreams into a bag and carry them into a fishing hut, you can't even buy such things, yet there are five shops in the Village and the selection is dizzying when things are at their best at midsummer. Perhaps it will never be possible to buy what matters most, no, of course not, that is unfortunately not the case, or, to put it better, thank God. They have finished emptying their bags and the contents lie on the bed. Three newspapers, two of them published in Reykjavík, coffee, rock candy, rye bread, sweet rolls from the German Bakery, two books from the library of the blind old sea captain – *Niels Juel, Denmark's Greatest Naval Hero* and Milton's *Paradise Lost* in the translation of Jón Þorlaksson – in addition to two books they had bought jointly at the Pharmacy from Dr Sigurður, *Travelogue of Eiríkur from Brúnum* and Jón Ólafsson's textbook of the English language. Sigurður has a pharmacy and bookshop in the same house, the books smelling so much of medicine that we are cured and freed from ailments simply by catching a whiff of them, tell me it's not healthy to read books. What do you want with this, asks the Custodian, Andrea, picks up the textbook and starts leafing through it. So we can say, I love you and I desire you in English, Bárður replies. That makes sense, she says, and sits down with the book. The boy came with three bottles of cure-all, Chinese Vital Elixir, one for himself, one for Andrea, the third for Árni, who hadn't arrived yet, same as Einar and Gvendur, they had planned to spend the day visiting various huts, rambling, as it's called. Pétur the skipper, on the other hand, spent the entire day in the hut, cleaning his waterproofs and rubbing them with fresh skate liver, mending his sea-shoes, went out once to the salting house with Andrea, they spread a sail over the ever-growing saltfish stack, it has grown so high that Pétur doesn't need to bend over at all while they're at it. They've been married for twenty years and now his waterproofs hang down below, hang among the fishing gear, a strong odour comes off them now but they will boy, and the mugs in Andrea's hands shake a bit as she suppresses a laugh. Einar clenches his fists and shakes them at the boy, hisses something so unclear that barely half of it can be understood, he is missing several teeth, his dark beard imposing, grown halfway over his mouth, his ragged, thin hair nearly grey, but then they drink their coffee. Each sits on his own bed and the sky darkens outside. Andrea turns up the light in the lamp, windows at both gables, one frames a mountain, the other the sky and sea, they frame our existence, and for a long time nothing is heard but the surge of the sea and the contented slurping of coffee. Gvendur and Einar sit together and share one of the newspapers, Andrea scrutinizes the English textbook, trying to enlarge her life with a new language, Pétur just stares at nothing, the boy and Bárður both have their own papers, now only Árni is missing. He had gone home the day before yesterday after they had finished clearing the landing, struck out through the downpour from the north, through frost and snow, couldn't see a thing but still managed to find the way, a six-hour walk home, he's so young that the woman pulls him in, Andrea had said, yes, follows his goddamn dick, said Einar, seemingly furious all of a sudden. I know that you neither believe it nor can imagine it, she then said, speaking to Einar yet glancing partly at her husband, but there are men who are a bit more than muscles and longing for fish and women's crotches.

Maybe Andrea knew about the letter that Árni had been carrying. The boy wrote it for him, and it wasn't the first time Árni had asked him to write a letter to his wife, Sesselja, she reads it when of things, Andrea and Pétur listen. Bárður and the boy lie head-to-toe on the bed, they read, close their ears, look up briefly when a ship sails into the fjord and in the direction of the Village, no doubt a Norwegian steam-powered whaling ship, it sails in with a rumble and a racket, as if complaining about its lot. And the goddamn merchants have raised the price of salt, Einar says, suddenly remembers the most important news and stops telling about Jónas, who has composed ninety-two verses about one of the custodians, some of them quite lewd but so well composed that Einar can't help but recite them twice, Pétur laughs but not Andrea, men seem generally inclined towards the coarser things in this world, whatever unveils itself in a rush, entirely, while women desire whatever needs to be chased, whatever reveals itself slowly. Raise the price of salt?! Pétur exclaims. Yes, those villains! Einar shouts, and his face darkens with anger. Soon we'll be better off selling the fish wet, straight from the sea, as soon as they're caught, Pétur says thoughtfully. Yes, Andrea says, because they want it that way, and that's why they raise the price. Pétur stares at nothing and feels melancholy spreading through his mind and consciousness without fully realizing its cause. If they stop salting the fish then it's finished for the stack out in the salt-ing house, then where are Andrea and I supposed to go, he thinks, why does everything need to change, it's not fair. Andrea has got to her feet, starts to tidy after the coffee, the boy looks up momentarily from Eiríkur's travel diary, they catch each other's eye, as sometimes happens, Bárður sunk in Milton's *Paradise Lost*, which Jón Þorlaksson translated long a year ago, made a special trip down to the next fjord in order to do so, rowed out to a smack and bought the boots as well as chocolate bars for the kids and Sesselja, the youngest started to cry when it finished its chocolate and was completely inconsolable. What is sweet through and through often makes us sad in the end. American halibut fishermen come here in March or April, catch halibut off Greenland but outfit their ships from here, buy provisions and salt from us and pay cash, they sell us rifles, knives, biscuits, but nothing comes even halfway close to the rubber boots. American rubber boots are more expensive than an accordion, their price practically amounts to the yearly wage of a female farm labourer, they are so expensive that Árni needed months on end of denying himself *brennivín* and tobacco to save enough to afford them. But they're worth it, Árni says, and wades through moors, he walks over streams but always has dry feet, trudges on, in wet and snow with bone-dry feet and the rubber boots certainly the best thing that has ever come from the American empire, they knock everything else sideways, and now you understand why it would have been unforgivable to drown in them. Unforgivable carelessness, Árni says, and kisses Sesselja and kisses the children and they kiss him, it's a thousand times better to kiss and be kissed than to fish in open cockleshells far out upon the sea. His wife watches him leave, don't let him drown, she whispers, doesn't want the children to hear, doesn't want to scare them; nor do we need to raise our voices when we pray for what is most important. She goes in, reads the letter again and now dares to have a better look at the words that have been crossed out, just something the boy was unhappy with, Árni had said, she peers at them for a long time and then manages to read them. There you are, Pétur says, because Árni has arrived in dry socks, they can go and bait the lines, will likely row out to fish tonight.

II

It's different sleeping on the open sea than here in the Village, at the head of the fjord, between high mountains, actually at the bottom of the world, and the sea sometimes becomes so passive that we go down to the foreshore to stroke it, but it's never passive beyond the huts, nothing seems able to ease the sea's swell, not even the still nights, the star-strewn sky. The sea floods into the dreams of those who sleep on the open sea, their consciousness is filled with fish and drowned companions who wave sadly with fins in place of hands.

Pétur always wakes up first. He is also the skipper and wakes when everything is still dark, barely after 2.00 a.m., but he never looks at the clock, and anyway it's kept downstairs, under some rubbish. Pétur goes out, looks up at the sky, and the density of the darkness tells him the time. He fumbles for his clothing, the stove doesn't burn at night and the cold of March has sifted its way through the thin walls. Andrea breathes heavily by his side, sleeps soundly, she is at the bottom of her dreams, Einar snores and clenches his fists in his sleep, Árni sleeps head-to-toe with him, the boy and Bárður do not move, the giant Gvendur so incredibly lucky to have his own bed yet it's too small for him, you're two sizes too big for the world, Bárður said once, and Gvendur became so sad that he needed to step away for a moment. Pétur puts on his sweater, his trousers, totters down and out into the night, a slow, gentle breeze from the east and the outlines of a few stars just visible, they twinkle with their age-old news, their thousands-of-years-old light. Pétur squints, waits until his drowsiness leaves him completely, until his dreams have vaporized and his senses gained clarity, stands bowed, crooked, like an incomprehensible beast, sniffs the air, peers into the dark clouds, listens, perceives messages in the wind, half grunts, half growls, goes in again, lifts the trapdoor with his black head, says, we're rowing, doesn't say it loudly yet it's enough, his voice reaches down into the deepest dreams, sunders sleep and they are all awake.

Andrea dresses beneath the bedcover, gets up and lights the stove and the lamp, it glows, a gentle light, and for a long time no-one says anything, they simply put on their clothes and yawn, Gvendur rocks sleepily at the edge of his bed, so muddleheaded on the border between sleep and waking that he doesn't know where he is. They scratch their beards, except for the boy, he's got nothing, one of the few who spends time scraping it off, of course not a great deal of work, it's both thin and sparse, you need some manliness, Pétur said once, and Einar had laughed. Bárður has a thick brown beard, trims it regularly, he's damned handsome, Andrea looks at him sometimes and then just to look, really, as we look at a beautiful picture, at the light over the sea. The coffee boils, they open their boxes, spread butter and pâté on rye bread with their thumbs, a lot of butter and pâté and the coffee is boiling hot and black as the darkest night but they put rock candy in it, if we could only put sugar into the night to make it sweet. Pétur breaks the silence, or rather the slurping, the smacking and the occasional fart, and says, the wind is from the east, gentle, slightly warm, but it'll turn to the north sometime today, not until later, so we'll row out deep.

Einar sighs happily. Row out deep, it's like a hymn in his ears. Árni says, yes, of course, he actually expected this, I'm sure we'll row out deep, he had said to Sesselja, who then said, oh, don't let the sea take you.

The fish had been slow to bite in the shallower fishing grounds before the bad-weather days and it would be natural to try the deeper ones now, they all reach into their boxes for another slice. Row deep, that means up to four hours of continuous rowing, the wind too quiet for the sail, and at least eight or ten hours out on the sea, maybe twelve, which means there are exactly twelve hours until they eat next, the bread is good, the butter is good and it's likely impossible to live without drinking coffee. They drink the last cup of coffee slowly, enjoy it, outside a half-dark night awaits them, it reaches from the bottom of the sea up to the sky where it kindles the stars. The sea breathes heavily, it is dark and silent, and when the sea is silent, everything is silent, even the mountain above them, alternately white and black. There is a dim light from gleam from the lamp reaches it, light that can illuminate a good line of poetry has surely achieved its purpose. His lips move, he reads the lines again and again, and each time the world inside him becomes a bit larger, expands. The boy has finished his coffee, shakes out his mug, puts it in his box, watches Bárður out of the corner of his eye, sees his lips move, affection passes through him, and yesterday returns with all the brightness and intense presence that accompanies Bárður, that accompanies friendship, he sits on the edge of the bed and yesterday is within him. He fumbles for the bottle of Chinese Vital Elixir, which is a powerful good digestive, a refreshing and strengthening medicine, which works well against tiresome wind in the intestines, heartburn, nausea, uneasiness in the diaphragm, everyone knows this, we read about it in the papers where it's confirmed by foreigners as well as Icelanders, doctors, parish administrators, sea captains, everyone recommends this elixir, it has saved lives, children at death's door after a bout of the flu have regained complete health after several spoonfuls, it also works perfectly for seasickness, five to seven tablespoonfuls before leaving shore and you're totally free from seasickness. The boy takes a drink from the bottle. Hell is being seasick in a sixereen out on the open sea, needing to work and many hours from shore. He takes another drink because seasickness returns, many times worse than before after long stretches on shore. Andrea has taken her dose against the cough that weighs her head down unnecessarily, drink the elixir and the discomfort disappears or never finds you. Our existence is a relentless search for a solution, what comforts us, whatever gives us happiness, drives away all bad things. Some travel a long and difficult road and perhaps find nothing at all, except for some sort of purpose, a kind of liberation or relief in the search itself, the rest of us admire their tenacity but have enough trouble ourselves simply existing, so we take cure-alls instead of searching, continually asking what is the shortest path to happiness, and we find the answer in God, science, *brennivín*, Chinese Vital Elixir.

They have all come outside.

There is a considerable amount of snow around the huts but the beach is black. They turn the boats over. Light work for twelve hands to put a sixereen onto its keel, a heavier task to overturn it, then twelve hands scarcely suffice, they need an additional six, at least, but the other crew is fast asleep, the bastards, resting their tired hands in a dream-world, they always head out to the deep-sea banks and thus never leave before dawn. Guðmundur will wake up soon, of course, the skipper called Guðmundur the Strict, his men have to be at the hut before 8.00 in the evening, the loafing and endless prattling poison in his veins, and they heed him uncondi-tionally, all of them giants, have made it alive through the storms of the world and are so insolent that they could kill a dog with their language but turn into modest, fearful fellows if Guðmundur gets riled. The Custodian there is called Guðrún, short and dainty, with such bright hair and radiant laughter that it is never completely dark where she is, she is the equivalent of many bottles of elixir, she is beautiful, she is frisky and her cheeks so white and convex that they can make one's heart ache, she sometimes dances a few peculiar steps and then something cracks inside the men in the hut, these rough and weathered men, affection and wild lust internal knots that are impossible to unravel. But Guðrún is Guðmundur's and they would rather cool off in the deadly cold sea than try anything with his daughter, are you crazy, even the Devil himself wouldn't dare touch her. She seems entirely unaware of her influence and perhaps that's the worst, unless it's the best in fact.

They work in silence.

Carry what needs to be carried down to the boat, the rigging, the baited lines, the waterproofs, the weather too mild to put them on immediately, the skin trousers reach up to under their arms, the wool in their sweaters well fulled, ahead of them three or four hours of heavy rowing. Each man with his own specific task during the night, if only existence were always so direct and easily readable, if only we could escape the uncertainty that reaches out over graves and death. But what softens uncertainty if death does not? The snow will soon become densely packed from the hut down to the black beach. Andrea comes out and empties the chamber pot, the ground is stony around the hut and receives the liquid, urine or rain, it disappears into the ground and it's just as well that the roof of Hell doesn't leak, unless one of the punishments is in fact to have wastewater and rain constantly pouring down on one. Andrea stands for a moment and watches them work, hardly a footstep of theirs can be heard, the sea sleeps, the mountain dozes and the sky is silent, no-one awake there, the hour no doubt approaching 3.00 and Bárður gives a sudden jump, disappears once more into the hut. Andrea shakes her head but also smiles weakly, knows he is standing on the ladder, reaches into the bed, opens *Paradise Lost* and reads the lines he wishes to memorize and recite for himself and the boy out on the sea, now comes evening,

> and a cowl the colour
> of dusk casts
> over all,
> accompanied by silence
> and already are
> beasts in burrows
> and birds in nests
> for the night
> reposed

Bárður had been the last one out. Sunk in a verse by a blind Englishman that a poor priest rewrote in Icelandic when time went by another name. He reads the verse again, shuts his eyes briefly and his heart beats. Words still seem able to move people, it is unbelievable, and perhaps the light is thus not completely extinguished within them, perhaps some hope yet remains, despite everything. But here comes the moon, sailing slowly into a

31

black hole in the sky with white light in its sails, it is just barely half, waxing to the left, yet the night will still be bright for a time. The light of the moon is of a different family than the light of the sun, it makes the shadows darker, the world more mysterious. The boy looks up, looks at the moon. It takes the moon just as long to make one rotation as to revolve around the Earth, and because of that we always see the same side, it is just over three hundred thousand kilometres away, it would take a very long time to row there in a sixereen, even Einar would be put off by the distance.

The boy's mother had written to him about the moon. About the distance to it, about its mysterious far side, but she never mentioned a sixereen in that context, nor Einar, didn't even know of his existence, neither his beard nor the anger that boils like an eternal engine inside him. But Einar isn't angry now. The tranquil moonlit night seeps into the six men and the woman watching them. No, Andrea isn't watching any longer, she has gone up to the hut, hurrying to meet Bárður in the narrow doorway. Am I crazy, thinks Andrea, there are twenty years between us! But why deny oneself the chance to gaze into such brown eyes on a March night, think about the soft and supple movements beneath his clothing, white, straight teeth between his lips, free from brown tobacco stains. Bárður doesn't chew tobacco, they're strange some of these young people, to deny themselves such delights as accompany tobacco. They meet in the doorway, his head full of poetry and loss of Paradise, oh, how beautiful you are, my poor thing, she says, and strokes his beard with both hands, then down his bare neck,

I missed him! is written in one of the letters she sent the boy, *of course I had you three but I still missed Björgvin every day, and even more in the evenings when you were asleep.* The months that he was away from home were packed with work, the struggle to live and to keep poverty at bay, while free time went into reading. *We were hopeless. We thought continuously about books, about being educated, became fervent, frantic, if we heard of some new and interesting book, imagined what it might be like, spoke about its possible contents in the evenings, after you'd gone to bed. And later we'd read it in turns, or together, when and if we managed to get hold of it, or a handwritten copy of it.* But what can we say, his father was out on a sixereen, they are common here, just over eight metres, and he was certainly not the only one to drown that night. That March night, the boy looks again at the moon and counts in his mind, ten years and seventeen days ago. No, no, two boats lost and both their crews, twelve lives, twenty-four hands groping in the sea, a south-easterly flared up and the sea drowned them all. A whole week passed before they received the dark tidings. Is it cruelty or comfort that he lived seven days longer in the minds of those most important to him, dead yet still alive? It was a neighbour who came and extinguished the light of the world. The boy sat on the floor with his legs stretched out in front of him, his sister between them, but his mother stood and stared straight ahead, her hands hung down at her sides, as if dead, Hell is having arms but no-one to embrace. The air quivered as if something great had been torn, then a crashing sound was heard when the sun fell and landed on the Earth.

People are alive, have their moments, their kisses, laughter, their embraces, words of endearment, their joys and sorrows, each life is a universe that then collapses and leaves nothing behind but a few objects that acquire attractive power through the deaths of their owners, become important, sometimes sacred, as if pieces of the life that has left us have been transferred to the coffee cup, the saw, the hairbrush, the scarf. But everything fades in the end, memories are wiped out after a time and everything dies. Where once was life and light are darkness and oblivion. The boy's father dies, the sea swallows him and never brings him back. Where are your eyes that made me beautiful, the hands that tickled the children, the voice that kept the darkness away? He drowns and the family is broken up. The boy goes to one place, his brother to another, five hours of vigorous marching between them, their mother and a sister just over a year old end up in a completely different valley. One day all four of them are lying in the same bed, it's crowded but it's good, almost the only good thing in the midst of the regret, then a seven-hundred-metre-high mountain rises between them, steep and barren, the boy still hates it, boundlessly. But it is so feeble to hate mountains, they are larger than we are, they stand in their places and do not move for tens of thousands of years while we come and go quicker than the eye can focus. Mountains, however, seldom stop letters. His mother wrote. She described his father so he wouldn't be forgotten, so he would live on in the mind of the son, a light by which to warm himself, a light to miss, she wrote to save her husband from oblivion. She heart is a hollow muscle that pumps blood through the body's blood vessels, the arteries, veins and capillaries that are nearly four hundred thousand kilometres long, reach the moon and just a touch out into the black space beyond it, it must be lonely there. Andrea stands between the boat and the hut, looking at them, her veins reach to the moon. The clock approaches 3.00 and they may not push out from the landing any earlier, there are laws, we'll follow the laws, especially those that make a bit of sense. Gvendur and Einar are already in the boat, seated on the fore thwart, only powerful and durable oarsmen sit there, the others take their places along the planking and wait for the trumpet to sound. Not, however, the one that old books and fairy tales say signals the Last Day, when we will all be called before the Great Judge, no, they simply wait for the trumpet that Benedikt will raise to his lips below the main huts when the clock strikes precisely 3.00. Benedikt has huge lungs and can blow hard, the signal to go carries to the brothers' huts even in a sharp headwind. The first winter after the rules prohibiting sea voyages before 3.00 in the morning took effect, Benedikt had simply blown quickly and unwaveringly, his only goal to hit a great note that carried far and proved the strength of his lungs, then he threw down the trumpet and joined the great race to be the first to go. But now, two years later, he has himself an old trumpet, bought from an English sea captain, and blows not simply to blow but emphasizes tenderness instead and tries to change the dark night sky into one of the melodies he heard from the merchant Snorri here in the Village, and Benedikt in the beard covering the lower part of his face, he holds onto the boat with both hands, every muscle taut. Einar squeezes his oar, Gvendur stares cheerfully into space, it's good just to exist. The boy looks at Einar over the gunwale, if any man could be a taut string at this moment it's Einar, Gvendur like a giant next to the string, a gentle, contented, submissive giant. They both work as farmhands for Pétur and have done so for a good ten years, although Pétur sometimes gets the feeling that the giant first heeds Einar and then him. Right, the bastard should start blowing any minute now, murmurs Árni again, slightly louder this time. Benedikt stands with legs spread in the middle of his boat about two kilometres from the brothers' huts, raises his trumpet to his lips, fills his lungs with dark night air and blows.

The note resounds above nearly three hundred skin-clad and impatient fishermen below the main huts, and carries far into the still night air. Andrea stretches, turns her head to hear better. Pétur, Árni and Einar have grown impatient, cursing Benedikt under their breath, while Bárður and the boy listen, try to learn the melody, its essence, something to improvise on during the long voyage and the life that will hopefully be longer yet. The giant Gvendur even closes his eyes furtively for a moment, music usually reminds him of something good and beautiful, and he feels it most when he's alone. He is, however, half afraid that Einar will see him, he certainly isn't happy about men closing their eyes while they're awake and Gvendur isn't one to offend Einar knowingly, life is tough enough as it is.

Right! shouts Árni when the sound dies out, and they push with all their might, as one man. The boat creeps off down the landing, the boy lets go, grabs the rollers that come out from under the keel, runs with them to the front of the boat and lays them in front of the prow. He's quick, we'll give him that, can run fast and so far in one shot that it's questionable whether the country would be large enough if he wanted to run somewhere at full tilt. The prow slips into the sea. Árni and Pétur are the last ones into the boat, they jump aboard out of the sea and then the rowing begins. Bárður and the boy share a thwart in the middle, the energy flows through their veins, they clench their teeth, six oars, the sea is quiet, no resistance, neither wind nor waves, the boat dashes forward, but when they have rowed for just under a minute and have torn themselves completely away from land, are on the sea, they pull in the oars, Pétur takes off his sou'wester, his woollen cap underneath it, takes that off as well, and recites the Seafarer's Prayer, the other five bow their heads with their sou'westers in their hands. The boat rises and falls, just like the throng of boats below the main huts, a scant minute after the great outburst released by Benedikt's note, when nearly three hundred men rushed shouting and screaming with just under sixty boats into the sea, but now the boats rise and fall in silence while the skippers pray. The voices ascend to Heaven with their message, their request, and it is simple: help us!

The sea is cold and sometimes dark. It is a gigantic creature that never rests, and here no-one can swim, except for Jónas, who works in the summers at the Norwegian whaling station, the Norwegians taught him how to swim, he is called either the Cod or the Sea-wolf, the latter more fitting, considering his appearance. Most of us have grown up here by the sea and have lived scarcely a day without hearing it, and the men pursued seamanship from the age of thirteen, that's the way it's been for a thousand years, yet no-one knows how to swim except Jónas, because he kisses up to the Norwegians. Still, we know a few other things, we know how to pray, know how to make the sign of the cross, we cross ourselves as soon as we wake, when we put on our waterproofs, we cross the fishing equipment, the bait, we cross each action, the thwarts upon which we sit we entrust to you, Lord, protect us with your loving kindness, silence the winds, still the waves that can become so terrifying. We place all of our trust in you, Lord, who are the beginning of all things and the end, because those who end up in the sea sink like stones and drown, even in dead calm and such a short distance from land that people standing with their feet firmly on the blessed Earth can see their expressions, their last ones before the sea claims their lives, or bodies, those heavy loads. We trust in you, Lord, who created us in your image, created the birds with wings so they could fly in the sky and remind us of freedom, created the fish with fins and tails so they could swim in the depths we fear. We can of course all learn to swim like Jónas, but Lord, would we not then be expressing our lack of faith in you, as if we thought ourselves capable of correcting something in creation? Besides, the sea is very cold, no man swims long in it, no, diminish. Their facial expressions are erased, she watches until they've become as one body taking the boat out to sea, into the night, in the direction of the fish that swim in the deep and simply enjoy existence. Andrea watches them, asks God to protect them, not to forsake them. She waits to return to the hut until she sees the throng of boats from the main huts round the cliff. It's pleasant to stand alone in the night, just above the foreshore, and see nearly sixty boats appear in the calm, see all of these men apply all of their strength to be the first to reach the fishing grounds and get to choose the best place, see them apply their utmost powers, which are however almost nothing in comparison with the sea, the fury of the wind, the wrath of the heavens, we trust in you, Lord, and your son, Jesus. She makes the sign of the cross, turns and notices her brother-in-law, Guðmundur. The brothers may no longer be speaking to each other, but they pay close attention to each other's activities. Then she wasn't alone, it was just a trick of the mind. Reality is complicated like that, because Andrea was completely alone in her thoughts and senses and her existence was based entirely on these, while several metres above her Guðmundur had been standing, watching the same thing as she was. Her anger flares but evaporates just as quickly, why should she get angry, Andrea thinks, completely surprised at herself, and she walks off in the direction of the hut, various tasks await her there and the Danish naval hero, if he weren't just another damned blatherer, another politician, did you know that incredibly few people can bear to wield power without remaining untarnished?

III

Guðmundur doesn't watch her but hears the door close. He looks out at the sea, the dark sea, and sniffs the air, a bit uncertain about the weather forecast, doesn't it seem as if there's a whiff of north-easterly behind the mountain, a sharp, even murderous wind direction? He doesn't move, the boats recede, they've started to vanish into the dark blue night, have started to spread out over the deep that opens up between the shores, between the mountains that rise precipitous and ancient. Guðmundur has a huge beard, it covers the entire lower part of his face, we never saw these men's chins, if one of them made the mistake of shaving, it would look as if he'd had a horrendous accident, a part of his personality cut off, nothing but half a man remaining. He stands motionless for a long time. Many minutes pass. It's healthy for a person to stand alone in the night, he or she becomes one with the tranquillity and discovers a kind of peace, which can however change without warning into painful isolation. It's still quite dark but there's a hint of a gleam in the east, so weak it's almost an illusion. But this gleam, imagined or not, dissolves Guðmundur's uncertainty, he is able to read the clouds over the white beach on the opposite side of the fjord, vague in the twilight, what his nose and ears couldn't tell him, that a north-easterly was on its way, likely gale-force, but would hardly reach them before midday. If they rushed to set out within the hour, they should be able to return before the sea could harm them, before the surf became murderous. He shudders, turns swiftly and takes long strides to his hut. These are such quick and unexpected movements in the calm that had befallen the night after the rush to launch the boats that they seem even to disturb the air surrounding the huts, as if causing it to quiver slightly, and Andrea looks up as she cleans the floor in the loft. Guðmundur tears open the door to the hut and shouts, rise and shine! we're rowing! He has a strong, sonorous voice and his men wake up immediately. They're out of bed before they can even blink, some still half asleep when their feet touch the floor. Guðrún lies in bed a few moments more, counting to a hundred, life is cosier under the cover than on the floor among the men, grunting in their coarse wool, yawning away their sleep and dreams, immediately eager to launch out onto the sea, to meet freedom and the fish.

Guðmundur's men are quick to come outside. They turn the boat over, almost a full metre longer than Pétur's boat, load it, don't forget to make the sign of the cross over everything they touch. They have rowed together for twenty years, started young fishing for shark during the years when no laws controlled deep-sea fishing and they could fish whenever it suited them, often during the blackest of midwinter days, when the darkness was so dense that one could draw a knife and carve one's initials into it and then the night would carry your name into morning. Some nights they lay for hours at a time above the sharks, in biting frost, far out at sea, and then it was as if the night would never pass and the east was heavy with darkness. The shark is always hungry and swallows everything, once Guðmundur's men found a dog in a shark's belly, the shark had eaten it the day before in a fjord fifty kilometres away, the dog had swum after its master's yawl, happy, tongue dangling, then it yelped suddenly and was gone, that's how dangerous it is to know how to swim.

Andrea cleans the floor in the loft, she thinks about the six men out on the sea in their yawl, she thinks about the moment with Pétur in the salting house the day before and then suddenly becomes so sad that she stands up, has a drop of coffee, sits down on the boy's bed, sighs quietly and reflexively strokes the cover of the book Bárður was reading. She reads the title out loud, opens the book and sees the letter Bárður had stuck into the middle of it, maybe to use as a bookmark. It is to Sigríður, three densely written pages. Andrea reads the first lines, which are burning hot with love, but is a little ashamed of herself, or just enough to stop reading. She closes the book again, looks to one side and sees Bárður's waterproof, and it's as if something cold touches her.

IV

They have been rowing for a long time and the sky is brightening. They have rowed out of the night and into the fragile morning. They have taken off their sou'westers. Little by little they lost sight of the other boats scattered over the wide expanse of the deep, the sea rolling, and they row further than the others and head towards a deep-sea fishing bank that Pétur knows of but has not visited for several years, they trust him, he knows more than all of them combined as far as cod are concerned, he thinks like a cod, Bárður once said, and it was difficult to know whether that was praise or derision, it can be difficult to figure Bárður out, but Pétur decided to take it as praise. They attack the oars and put more distance between themselves and the land. It can hurt to move further away from land, it's as if one were rowing towards loneliness. The boy watches the mountains diminish, they seem to sink into the sea. The mountains threaten us when we're on land, gather storms unto themselves, kill people by hurling stones at them, wipe out towns with avalanches and mudslides, but the mountains are also a protecting hand, they foster us and embrace

48

the boats that row into the fjords, but nothing protects the fishermen who row far except their prayers and ingenuity. They've started to grow weary although Einar still takes delight in the task, still has a gleam in his eyes. Bárður breathes shallowly at the boy's side. We two aren't born for seamanship, he had said yesterday, in the German Bakery, over a cup of coffee and a sweet roll.

The coffee in the bakery is somehow cleaner, free of grounds. Might as well get used to the luxury, the boy had told Bárður, but then the bakers, husband and wife, started to argue in German in the back. Their disagreements were quick to explode, and in a short time they were shouting at each other, but suddenly everything went dead calm and silent in the bakery, then a suppressed giggle could be heard, followed by the smacking sounds of passionate kisses. The two female shop assistants went about their work and pretended not to hear, but Bárður glanced with a smile at the boy and it was incredibly good to be alive. There they sat in the bakery, celebrating the future, Bárður having secured them summer work at the shop run by Leó, his father, a close acquaintance of the Factor, who was called Jón and who has trouble standing still, shuffles his feet as he speaks, shuffles them as he listens, continually licks his lips with the tip of his tongue. Jón would be nothing without his wife, Tove, Bárður had explained, she's Danish, some call her the Frigate and you would understand the name if you saw her come sailing down the street. The world becomes considerably easier if you have her on your side, she appreciates hard work:

you just need to stick to your job and everything will be fine. It's also a dream job, no hard slogging, you're not exhausted by the end of the day and there's not a stain to be seen on your clothing, you don't even need to wash your hands!

The sea is wide and very deep and the boy has never rowed out so far.

This is actually unnecessarily far.

Just a thin piece of wood between them and drowning, he will never get used to this, and here the wind blows harder. The waves rise higher, the sea becomes heavier. Yet this is no weather to speak of, and they row. They pull hard, their muscles knit, wait for us, cod, we're coming. He looks at Pétur's back, there is no resemblance between him and his niece, Guðrún, are you crazy, it's like comparing a summer's night and sleet. It's a shame it's so difficult to talk to her, it's nigh impossible because he frequently loses both his tongue and his courage when she looks at him, and in any case Guðmundur would order the men to tear him apart and use him for bait if he tried something other than look at and admire her. The land continued to sink into darkness and sea but soon the light will come from the east. They see a few stars, the clouds are of various types, blue, almost black, light and grey and the sky ever-changing, like the heart. Bárður pants and mumbles something, in snatches because of the strain … cowl casts … colour of dusk. All of their hearts beat fast. The heart is a muscle that pumps blood, the abode of pain, loneliness, joy, the one muscle that can keep us awake at night. The abode of uncertainty: whether we will wake again to life, whether it will rain on the hay, whether the fish will bite, whether she loves me, whether he will come over the heath to speak the words, uncertainty about God, about the purpose of life but no less the purpose of death. They row and their hearts pump blood and uncertainty about fish and life but not about God, no, because then they would scarcely venture out in a little cockleshell, in an open coffin, onto the sea, which is blue on the surface but pitch-black beneath. God is all-embracing in their minds. He and Pétur are likely the only ones whom Einar respects in this world, sometimes Jesus, but that respect was not as uncon-ditional, a man who offers his other cheek wouldn't last long in the mountains here. Árni rows and sometimes becomes one with the exertion, for a long time thinks nothing but then Sesselja comes to mind, and the children, three living children and one dead, Árni rows and thinks about the houses, the livestock, the parish, he plans to become a town council member within three years, a man has to have a goal in life, otherwise you get nowhere and decay. There is power in the twelve practised arms but the boat seems hardly to have moved at all, the waves toss and turn all around them, there is no violence in them but still they are large and block any sort of view, there is an ocean in these waves and the boat is just a piece of wood, the men sit on the wood and trust in God. Bárður and the boy are, however, not as confident as the rest. They are young and have read unnecessarily much, their hearts pump more uncertainty than the others', and not just about God, because the boy is also uncertain about life, but particularly about

51

himself in life, about his purpose. He thinks about Guðrún and his uncertainty doesn't lessen because of it. Guðrún has bright eyes, they are so bright that they vanquish night, he thinks between oar strokes, and is pleased with this sentence, repeats it and memorizes it to tell Bárður later today, when they have firm ground beneath their feet and where it is considerably more distant to the next man than here in the boat. He looks at Pétur's back, hears Gvendur breathe slowly and gigantically behind him. Eyes so bright that they vanquish night, he repeats to himself, and a line Bárður had read from *Paradise Lost* last evening comes to him there in the boat: nothing is sweet to me, without thee. The boy murmurs these two sentences, eyes so bright that they vanquish night, nothing is sweet to me, without thee – but then starts to think about her breasts. Tries as hard as he can to think instead about the night, about uncertainty, but it's useless, his head is filled with images and words and he has an erection. In fact it's good at first, but then it isn't good any more and he is deadly ashamed of himself. Now he can no longer look at Guðrún, it's finished, he has lost her, I should jump overboard like a shot, nothing is sweet to me, without thee, pants Bárður, as if to punish him. Quotes from the book the blind sea captain had loaned him. They had stopped at Geirþrúður's café on their way out of the Village; now we'll go visit Geirþrúður, Bárður had said as he finished his cup of coffee at the bakery, the smacking of kisses has fallen silent but the baker has begun to sing in German, an importunate song, in a high, soft voice.

There is considerable traffic on the streets of the Village and some of the houses rise high above them.

The boy felt slightly smaller because of the bustling life, the houses and the name Geirþrúður. They stopped first at Tryggvi's Shop, and then to see Magnús the shoe-smith, where Bárður had his feet measured and ordered knee-high boots for the spring and summer here in the Village. Don't be afraid of Geirþrúður, said Bárður afterwards as they were approaching the Café, she won't eat you, or at most just one of your arms. And what Bárður said was absolutely right, she didn't eat the boy, but perhaps mainly because she wasn't there, or at least didn't come into the Café, where they stopped for around half an hour. These were rather long minutes for the boy, feeling insecure about Helga, Geirþrúður's right hand, about her grey, searching eyes, fearful of the sea captain and his hoarse voice, his cutting words and those dead eyes beneath his high, wrinkled forehead that contains remarkable thoughts, or should have done, must do, because he owns at least four hundred books, Bárður had assured him. Bárður who seemed right at home there, had a laugh, introduced the boy, my friend, too gifted for the fish, and the word *friend* was so warm that the boy felt a little better. The mocking remarks of the three fishermen who sat over bottles of beer didn't touch him, he understands their language after having rowed through almost three winter fishing seasons. The overland postman, Jens, was also there. Big, drunk, newly arrived from his monthly trip from Reykjavík, a six- to eight-day journey. Bárður and the boy had seen the boxes and bags of post in the Café's entryway. Of course Jens should have taken the post directly to Dr Sigurður, where it is sorted and then handed over to the sub-postmen who carry it to the farms and fjords all around, but Jens couldn't care less about regulations, he also bears half a grudge against Sigurður, and in any case it's much better to sit in Geirþrúður's café and drink as much beer as he can and as he can afford, nor is Sigurður too good to come fetch the post himself. Jens had given the boy a quick look but otherwise didn't pay any attention to him or Bárður, occupied as he was with speaking to Skúli, editor of the *Will of the People* newspaper. The boy had seen Skúli once before, but from a distance, had stared at this tall, well-dressed man. It must be wonderful to work as a writer for a newspaper, a thousand times better than fishing. Skúli had papers in front of him and was writing down something dictated to him by the postman. The next paper will be chock-full of fresh news because Jens has walked and ridden the whole way from Reykjavík, with news from the capital and from abroad, along with all the little bits of news he has collected on his long journey. Jens stops at many farms, there are many mouths that wish to tell something, gossip, ghost stories, speculations on the distance between two stars, between life and death, we are what we say, but also what we do not say. The blind captain, Kolbeinn, is silent about many things and luckily had no interest in the boy, he only spoke to Bárður, take this book about Juel for Andrea, he said, and this one here is for you. Kolbeinn put one hand on the large book before him, *Paradise*

Lost, printed in 1828, you see I trust you, he said to Bárður, almost cruelly, was silent for a moment, as if contemplating these words, *you see*, continued to speak about the book, it will change your life, which could certainly use a change.

Nothing is sweet to me, without thee.

Milton was blind like the sea captain, an English poet who lost his sight in old age. Composed his poems in darkness and his daughter wrote them down for him. We thus bless her hands, but hopefully they had a life apart from the poems, hopefully they were able to hold something warmer and softer than a slender dip pen. Some words can conceivably change the world, they can comfort us and dry our tears. Some words are bullets, others are notes of a violin. Some can melt the ice around one's heart, and it is even possible to send words out like rescue teams when the days are difficult and we are perhaps neither living nor dead. However, words are not enough and we become lost and die out on the heaths of life if we have nothing to hold but a dip pen. Comes evening, and a cowl casts, over all. Lines written in darkness that never left his eyes, written down by a woman's hand, translated into Icelandic by a priest who had excellent vision but was sometimes so poor that he didn't have paper to write on and then was forced to use the sky over Hörgárdalur Valley for a page.

Right! Pétur says loudly.

Right!

The first word heard in the boat for nearly four hours.

They stop rowing at once.

They breathe as heavily as the sea beneath them.

Most of the mountains have sunk completely, but the outlines of two peaks appear dimly and it is by them that Pétur steers, the boat is above the fishing bank, where the depth is not as great and the sea is not as frightfully dark below.

Right! and Árni and Pétur have pulled in the oars.

One word, which is, however, scarcely a word and is in general completely useless, we scarcely say, right! when we dream about purpose, yearn for lips, touch, we scarcely sigh, right! when we reach orgasm, we don't say, right! when someone abandons us and our hearts harden to stone. But Pétur doesn't need to say more. The men don't need words out here on the open sea. The cod have no interest in words, not even adjectives such as *splendid*. The cod have no interest in any words, and yet have swum nearly unchanged through the seas for 120 million years. Does this tell us something about language? We might not need words to survive; on the other hand, we do need words to live.

Pétur says, right!, casts the buoy overboard and starts to set the first line together with Árni.

The other four row the line out. This long stretch of rope with countless hooks onto which they threaded the bait during the evening, six lines, one for each man, Pétur's line laid first. He and Árni make the sign of the cross over each line before setting it so that nothing evil comes up from the deep, but what could that be?

The depths of the sea are innocent of all evil, they are just life and death, while there would certainly be a need to make the sign of the cross over the lines not just once but at least ten thousand times if we were to sink them into the depths of the human soul. The easterly breeze is growing steadily stronger, becoming more north-easterly. The temperature drops. Slowly, however, and they are still quite warm after the rowing, a warmth that doesn't completely leave the four who row out the line, the other two are cold but don't show it and in that way prove their strength, which is perhaps no strength at all but simply fear of others' opinions. People are sometimes ridiculous. The lines sink one after the other down into the cold blue sea, lie there in silence and the darkness of the deep, waiting for fish, preferably cod.

The six men wait in the boat for the fish that have swum the seas for 120 million years. Animal species have come and gone but the cod has swum its own course, humanity is just a short span in its life. The cod swims its whole life with a wide-open mouth, so gluttonous that it's second to none, except humans of course, eats everything it can catch and never gets enough, the boy once counted 150 full-grown capelin inside a medium-sized cod and was scolded severely for wasting so much time on such a thing. The cod is yellow and enjoys swimming, is always on the lookout for food, very little that is remarkable occurs in its life and a line that sweeps down with bait on a hook is considered great news, it is a huge event. What's this? the cod ask each other, finally something new, says one, and bites immediately, and then all of the others hurry to bite as well, because none wish to stand apart, it's excellent to hang around here, says the first out of the side of his mouth, and the others agree. Hours pass, then movement, then everything starts moving, they're all pulled away, some great power pulls them up, upwards and upwards in the direction of the sky, which soon breaks and opens onto another world full of peculiar fish.

They have set all the lines and the wait begins.

The long wait for the fish to bite. Two hours of doing nothing. Two hours in an open coffin out on the Polar Sea. In frost, rising wind. Now it's only Gvendur and Einar who have work to do. They do not let go of the oars, do not get a break from them until they reach land and the freedom of the sea is behind them, unless the wind is favourable for the sail, then they rest while the boat sails, Pétur steers and the sixereen turns into an elegant ship. Oh yes, those are good moments, even beautiful, a coffin becomes a ship that cleaves the waves, the men doze and their minds fill with dreams.

Gvendur and Einar row against the current to hold the boat steady near the buoy. The dark colour of night sinks slowly before the daylight, very slowly, it is still half-dark above their heads, a star here and there in breaks in the heavy, low-lying clouds that gradually fill the sky. Pétur stoops for the whey keg, removes the cork, takes a long drink, hands it to Árni, and they all drink in the same way, fill their mouths with whey and are refreshed. The temperature drops. This will be a cold wait but so what? They have waited over lines in colder weather than this, and have waited in more wind, so much so that it took four men to keep the boat in place. They have waited in so much darkness that Pétur needed to hold fast to the rope tied to the buoy so as not to let it slip from the boat and be lost, held fast to the rope but feared to his bones that the Devil was lurking in the night, holding onto the other end. Yet it would never cross his mind to let go, because the worst thing in this world is without doubt letting one's lines slip away, losing them, having to leave them behind, having to flee to shore in consternation before the fury can seize the boat, before the waves grew larger and broke over it, precisely as heavy as death. But the world is varied, there are storms and there are calms, and it was gloriously calm when they last rowed out, half a month ago. The world slept, the sea was a mirror that rose and fell. They had seen every crack and crevice in the mountains many kilometres from the boat and the sky arched over them like the roof of a church, the roof that protects us. The six men had been silent, humble and thankful for their existence. But it isn't natural for a person to feel thankful or humble for long: some had started thinking about tobacco and forgotten eternal life. Bárður and the boy had leaned back a bit and looked at the sparkling sky that makes us humble and powerful at once and seems sometimes to speak to us. What it says carefully cleanses old wounds.

But there are no stars now, not on this voyage. Not any longer. They have all disappeared behind the clouds that thicken overhead, bringing bad weather. Day is approaching, the wind grows stronger and colder, born of ice that fills the world behind the horizon, we shall not row in that direction, Hell is the cold. They throw on their waterproofs, because even though their sweaters are well fulled the arctic wind slips easily through them, and it certainly doesn't help that they're drenched in sweat. They all grab their waterproofs, all except for Bárður, he grabs nothing, his hand stiffens in the empty air and he curses loudly. What? asks the boy. Damned waterproof, I forgot it, and Bárður curses more, he curses having focused unnecessarily on memorizing lines from *Paradise Lost*, so focused that he forgot his waterproof. Andrea has surely already discovered this and fears for him shivering there in the cold, defenceless against the arctic wind. This is what poems can do to us. You're such an idiot, says Einar, and he grins, but Pétur says nothing and even appears to avoid looking at Bárður, who strings together all the curse words life has taught him, and they are many. Curse words are little pieces of coal and can heat things, but words unfortunately do little to keep out the arctic wind, it slips through and into the flesh, a decent windbreaker is many times better and more important than all the poems in the world. The boy and Bárður sit opposite each other astride the thwart, start to slap their palms together, first slowly, then as fast as they can, continuing until a decent heat has been produced in Bárður, while the boy has become sweaty and breathless. The heat, however, quickly leaves Bárður, who tries punching himself to generate heat, now I'll get sick, he thinks resentfully, will no doubt miss out on the next voyage, miss out on delivering the fish to the shop, miss out on the fish, hell, he curses, it's bad to miss out on the fish. Fish are not just a group of vertebrates with cold blood, living in water and breathing through gills, fish are much more than that. Most Icelandic settlements were built of cod bones, they are the pillars beneath the arched roof of dreams. Pétur dreams of becoming rich, tearing down the old farm and building a wooden house with windows, that would make Andrea happy and she could certainly use it, in fact it seemed as if something bad had happened between them. Yet Pétur doesn't know what it could be, he is, to tell the truth, helpless, he hasn't changed, always works at everything conscientiously, never gives himself a break, but why does he sometimes feel as if he is losing her, is life betraying him? But he can't put a finger on any particular event, there is nothing that supports this suspicion, except for the feeling that something in the air is working against him and raising a wall between them, creating distance. This suspicion sometimes turns into pure indisposition, depression touches him and takes the power from his arms, makes his head heavier, but rarely here on the sea, here he is happy, here he can overcome everything, and next to him sits Árni, the best deckhand Pétur has ever had. Árni also dreams of wooden houses, dreams of improving his fields, levelling tussocks, buying soft red fabric in Tryggvi's Shop at the end of the fishing season, along with toys for the children. He who has no dreams is in danger. Gvendur dreams of American boots and often eyes Árni's. Einar plans to buy a jacket and a chequered cap at the end waterproofs. Pétur starts humming, low and incoherently, relaxes his vocal cords, and when they are warm and flexible enough he starts reciting and the others perk up their ears. At first it's verses about horses, verses about fishing voyages, about heroism and derring-do on the sea. But heroism and horses don't do much against the cold, he changes course, starts reciting ambiguous verses that quickly turn obscene. Pétur knows a great many such verses, they number in the dozens, perhaps the hundreds. He has moved to another thwart and sits foremost in the boat, clad in his waterproof and large, thick woollen mittens, a woollen cap under his sou'wester, his cap reaches down to his eyelids, only his eyes, nose, part of his cheeks and mouth are visible, his beard hides the rest, it hides his expression and is likely the reason why he appears indomitable as he rocks back and forth and chews his tobacco. The verses gush out of him. As if to exorcise the arctic cold itself. The verses become steadily more raw, more violent, and Pétur is transformed. He is no longer a silent, serious skipper, the work-horse, something ancient and dark awakens in him, this is no longer poetry that wells up from within him, poetry is for laggards and schoolmen, this is a primitive force, a language with deep roots in a dim subconscious, sprung from a harsh life and ever-present death. Pétur grows burning hot and he rocks rhythmically on the thwart, slaps his hands now and then on his thigh when the rhyming words become so heavy that it is difficult for the human body to handle them, because the human body is delicate, it cannot bear the impact of large rocks, cannot bear avalanches,

63

the stinging cold, cannot endure loneliness, cannot endure rhyming words heavy with antiquity, saturated with lust, and this is why Pétur slaps his thigh, to bring the words forth, and the five men start in surprise, everyone bound by this primitive power streaming from their skipper. Einar's eyes are stretched wide with black happiness, Gvendur breathes through his mouth, Árni does not take his eyes off Pétur, Bárður's eyes are half closed, he does not listen to the words but rather to their sound, the sound in the voice, and thinks, the Devil himself, where does this old bugger get such power!? The boy swings between rapture and antipathy, he stares at a fifty-year-old man shovelling out obscene verses, what is Pétur but an old man and what are these verses but ribaldry? But in the next breath Pétur changes again, into something ancient, and the sound of the words rips into the boy. He curses himself, curses Pétur, he sits there in the midst of five men in a yawl on the Polar Sea, with frost all around, swinging between rapture and antipathy. Pétur has taken off his sou'wester, he has been sweating, has set aside one of his mittens, his large hand seems to be clenched around some of the words, he stares at nothing, focused, and tries not to think of Andrea, stay longer, she sometimes asks in the salting house, up on the saltfish stack that is getting higher, it will soon be so high that he will no longer be able to stand to do the deed, go slowly, she says, that's good, and she moves her legs further apart, both to enjoy him, to feel him better, but also so he doesn't hurt her, but the heat in her words and the legs that spread further apart become too much, everything bursts inside

64

Pétur, he shudders and clenches his teeth but Andrea looks away instinctively, as if to hide the disappointment, even the sadness, that shows on her face, and then there is silence in the salting house and Andrea avoids looking at her husband. At that very moment, in the midst of his pleasure in the power of verses, Pétur looks up. The power, the magic, the lust subside unexpectedly, turn to nothing, are sucked out of him and disappear when the fear of losing her seeks him out and fills every cell. Lose her where, he doesn't know, has never gone to the heart of that question, but what does he have, and what is life? Yes, it is this boat, the earth with its houses and creatures, and then Andrea. Thirty years with her. He knows no other life. If she were to disappear, he would lose his balance, he realizes that now, completely unexpectedly this conclusion stands before him, the verse dies on his lips and Pétur seems to collapse.

Einar curses softly. He knows the set of verses that ebbed out and had been waiting eagerly for the last stanzas. The unexpected silence brings the world back to them. Brings the frost, the wind, the rising waves and the snowflakes, because the swirling snowfall has drawn closer. Bárður rubs his arms furiously, the boy turns so he can rub his friend's chest and back simultaneously, Einar and Gvendur fight the waves, Árni avoids looking at Pétur, who is so unlike himself, sits there and appears to be waiting for someone to throw him overboard like something useless. The boat rises and falls. The seasickness that has plagued the boy so little on the voyage, he having blessed the Chinese Vital Elixir so often in his mind, now returns, yet is still mild, a qualm he should be able to work off when they start to haul in the lines, that is if they start sometime, if time has not abandoned them, left them behind on the Polar Sea. Pétur shakes himself, he shakes himself like an animal, tears himself away from the numbness, the surrender, the fear, and says: let's row to the buoy.

Árni, Bárður and the boy straighten up, but Einar and Gvendur turn the boat around and row hard the short distance to the buoy, because now they shall haul in fish, now they shall haul it up from the depths that keep life in us, improve homes and amplify dreams. Bárður fastens the spool onto the rowlock, his job is to haul in the line, needed for this work are strength and stamina, of which he has a considerable amount. Pétur leans slightly over the side, looks down into the sea, waits with the gaff in his right hand, they start with his line, the skipper's line. They quiver with expectation. Bárður pulls, down in the deep the line moves, the cod rise to the surface and receive a rude reception. Pétur gaffs the fish on board, shortly afterwards Árni bleeds them with one swift movement and they never swim again through the dark blue depths with wide-open mouths, swallowing everything smaller than themselves, those moments of delight are behind them and death takes over, but we do not know where death takes them, should the eternal sea exist somewhere behind time, full of deceased fish, some long extinct here on earth? The fish has cold blood and is perhaps not particularly sensitive concerning life and death, sweater. The wind blows over the Polar Sea, strengthening every minute and spitting out snowflakes. Gvendur and Einar now need to use all their strength to hold the boat reasonably steady, the waves rise around them, the land is long gone, the horizon gone, there is nothing in the world any longer but six men in a cockle-shell, pulling fish and dreams from the cold deep. Pétur holds firm, hooks the fish aboard, looks first at Bárður and then at the weather around them, Árni and Bárður have started to haul in the fifth line, Gvendur's, he holds tightly to his oar, so huge next to Einar but small and frightened inside because it must be awful to drown, and the Polar Sea no longer cares for this boat, about this piece of wood with its men, and now the storm breaks. The snowfall thickens. Yet it was hardly possible to call this a snowfall. The wind whips the snowflakes into the men's faces, forcing them to squint, or rather to look away. The waves break around the boat, seawater dashes over them, not much but it only takes a little to drench a man who leaves his waterproof on land, Bárður gasps for breath. And at almost the same moment Árni looks at Pétur, who nods, throws the gaff into the pile of fish, just under two hundred fish, Árni reaches for the knife, cuts Gvendur's line, much of which they had already hauled in, partly bent over the work, neither sitting nor standing, it's high time, sighs the boy, who has vomited twice, vomited the whey, vomited the rye bread he ate in the night, some into the boat, some into the sea, the rest taken by the wind. The snowfall thickens around them and diminishes the world, their visibility is limited to just a few metres, and the only thing they see are rising waves, deepening troughs. The boat is lifted, it plunges, Bárður's sweater has turned into a byrnie of ice, he sits down on a thwart, plunks himself down, punches himself furiously. The boy tries to tear himself away from his seasickness, which continues to grow stronger despite the Chinese Vital Elixir that is a world-famous and highly scientific product, hangs rather than sits on the thwart and rubs his friend weakly, offers to loan him his waterproof but Bárður shakes his head, the boy's waterproof is far too small, nor would it improve matters to have them both soaked. Damn, damn, damn, mutters Bárður. What about my line?! Einar shouts, looking madly at Pétur and Árni. We can't wait any longer! Pétur shouts back, a space of only three metres between them, but if one wants to be heard here on the Polar Sea, one must shout, scream, yet it's not certain that this will suffice. Einar shouts, he twists his head as if in torment, as if to calm the violence that threatens to explode his head, then clenches his teeth with all his might and manages to hold back the words that howl inside him. Pétur is skipper, his words are law, whoever disagrees can go elsewhere, but it's still a damned shame, makes Einar so angry that he literally sees blood when all of the lines but his are hauled in, heavy with fish, this is the blackest injustice, this is pitch-black Hell. More than three hours of intense rowing, another three hours pushing against the wind and tide and what does one get, nothing, the fish left behind down in the sea, hanging on their hooks. Einar looks with murderous eyes at Bárður trying to punch away the cold, and at the deathly pale boy rubbing his friend, it isn't that the wind tears apart and throws into their faces. The boy continues to punch the frost off the sail and the boat, it's easier for him to breathe. The certainty that Bárður will not let the frost defeat him gives him increased strength, sweet is the breath of morn, and for a time he forgets everything but the effort to punch frost and snow from the sail, except for the fight for life, but when he next looks over, Bárður has crawled into the bow and lain down there. The boy totters, half-crawls and pushes Einar to one side so he can get to Bárður, Einar shouts in his ear, do you want us all to be killed, you damned piss-pup! Because the man who doesn't do his job puts everyone in danger, but so what, there lies Bárður, has drawn his knees up to his chest and hooked his arms around them. The boy crouches next to him and calls out, Bárður! He calls the name that means more than all the other names in the world combined, more than a boat with two hundred fish, comes so close that he breathes on Bárður's brown eyes. Bárður looks back at him, completely expressionless because the cold has paralysed the muscles in his face, but still he looks. The boy's collar is grabbed. Einar pulls him up roughly, the boy looks across the boat, Pétur and Árni shout at them but he hears nothing, the only thing that can be heard is the din of the wind. The boy looks at Einar and then strikes at him with ice-cold fury, hits him on the chin. Einar jerks back at the blow, but no less at the fury that makes the boy unrecognizable, he falls to his knees, rips off his waterproof, tries futilely to put it on Bárður, rubs Bárður's face, punches his shoulders and breathes on his eyes because life is there, he shouts, he punches

72

more, and he rubs harder but it makes no difference, it is useless, Bárður has stopped looking, there is no longer any expression in his eyes. The boy has taken off his mittens and rubs the cold face of his friend, stares into his eyes, breathes on them, whispers, says something, strokes his cheeks, he slaps them and he shouts and waits and whispers but nothing happens, the connection between them has broken, the cold has claimed Bárður. The boy looks over his shoulder, at the four men fighting for their lives, fighting united, looks back at Bárður who is alone, nothing can touch him any more, except the cold. Nothing is sweet to me, without thee.

V

It is ridiculously good to have solid ground beneath one's feet. Then you haven't drowned and can have something to eat after twelve hours on the Polar Sea within the gales and ragged snowfall. Eat many slices of rye bread with a mound of butter and pâté and drink pitch-black coffee with brown sugar. It doesn't get much beter than that. The hunger having started to gnaw at the men's insides, the exhaustion quivering in their muscles, at such a moment coffee and rye bread are Heaven itself. And then, when the catch has been worked, fresh-boiled fish with suet gravy. Happiness is having something to eat, to have escaped the storm, come through the breakers that roar just beyond the land, to hit them at precisely the right second required to sail through them, otherwise the surf topples the boat or fills it and then six men who cannot swim are in the sea with two hundred dead fish, the catch destroyed and a considerable likelihood that the men are drowned, but Pétur is a genius, he knows the moment, they slide through and have escaped.

Gvendur and Einar jump overboard, land in the knee-deep

74

sea, Guðmundur and one of his crew splash out to meet them. They did not row, Guðmundur decided not to go at the last minute, the very last, two of his crew sat in their waterproofs in the boat, the others had started to push when Guðmundur called it off, there was a play of colours out on the horizon that he did not like. And those on shore do not passively watch the boats land but instead lend a hand, there is a law beyond man-made laws because here it is a question of life and death, and most choose the former. Life also has an advantage over death in the way you have some idea of what you're dealing with, death on the other hand is the great uncertainty, and there is little more antipathetic to human beings than uncertainty; it is the worst of all.

Four men from Guðmundur's crew stand at the winch along with Gvendur and Einar and haul the boat up the landing, the others push, out beyond them crashes the fuming surf, even further out rages the storm. The weather is considerably better here, although there is a whine in the mountains above the huts and the wind is so strong that Andrea has to stand with her legs spread and sometimes to lean into it. The coffee is ready inside the hut and she stands there, leans into the wind, doesn't understand what's going on inside her, should have gone down to the boats, pushed the final metres, picked two fish from the catch to boil, then gone with the men up to the hut where they would sit happily over the aroma of coffee and old bread from their boxes, happiness can be found in small things. Those are good times, sitting among the men, asking about the voyage, sensing the smell of the ocean filling the loft, yet she stands there, unmoving. She squints, tries to protect her eyes from the ragged snowfall. Something is wrong. She feels it. And the same sense of foreboding she felt that morning, when her eyes fell on Bárður's waterproof, swells up inside her. It's as if she dare not move, as if the slightest movement would confirm her worst fear.

A living body is amazing. But at the same time as the heart ceases to beat, no longer pumps blood, and memories and thoughts no longer sparkle within the skull, it ceases to be amazing and turns into something for which we would prefer not to have to find words. Best let science do that. And then the ground. Andrea squints, turns her head away from the obtrusive snowflakes, finally comes up with the idea of counting the men. There are Gvendur and Einar at the winch, Pétur holds onto the prow, there is Árni, there is the boy, and now she sees that their movements are heavy, not from fatigue but from something entirely different, and Bárður is nowhere to be seen. Where is Bárður, she says involuntarily, asks the wind, asks the snowflakes, but neither replies, they do not need to, the wind just blows, it comes and is as quickly gone and the snowflakes are born of the heavens, that is why they are white and shaped like angels' wings. The heavens have never needed to explain anything, they arch high over our heads, over our lives, and are always as distant, we never come close to them whether we are standing on the roof of a house or on a mountain, try to chase them down with words or in vehicles. Andrea gives a start, as if she were going to take her first step, and then another, start walking, start striding, run down to the boat, down to the men who have finished dragging the boat ashore, the weather quite nasty but still not so bad that they need to secure the boat any further, not yet, because the storm is out at sea, two elements that drown the humans who risk them. Now they should set off for the hut, find happiness in the coffee, pleasure in the rye bread, the pâté, the butter, delight in the short rest, and Guðmundur should be plodding off to his own hut so as not to remain any longer than necessary under the same sky as his brother, dammit, someone should at least be moving, someone other than the continual wind, the snowflakes from the heavens. The men at the winch straighten up and look down into the boat. Those who pushed or pulled stand motionless, awkward, hands at their sides, stand like that for a long time, surely many minutes or hours, Andrea feels, but it is scarcely more than a few seconds. The hours are numerous and the clock seldom measures the time that passes inside us, the real lifetime, and because of this many days can fit into a few hours, and vice versa, and numbers of years can be an imprecise measure of a man's lifetime, he who dies at forty has perhaps actually lived much longer than he who dies at ninety. A few seconds or hours; the boy has heaved himself into the boat. He crouches down in the bow, then he rises slowly and has something large in his arms, something larger than a cod, even larger than a king cod, since this is not a cod but a man, the boy screams something and finally the lethargy falls away from the others. Árni is aboard in one movement, Gvendur and Einar come down the landing, and they take hold of Bárður and head towards the hut. It's almost as if the ground bends beneath the weight, yet it is hard with frost, rocks and millions of years, but a dead man is so much heavier than one who lives, the sparkling memories have become dark, heavy metal. No-one says anything. Guðmundur and his men stand motionless. They have taken off their woollen caps. Guðrún comes out the door, sees and then looks as if someone has punched her with a hard fist. Andrea has come into the hut, rushes up and then down again with *brennivín*, sweeps everything off the baiting table, they come in, lay Bárður on the table and the mountains above the huts whine. He lies with open eyes, stares upwards, ice-cold and yet does not want *brennivín*, wants nothing at all because he no longer is anything. Except for uncertainty. The cold had reached his heart, entered it and then everything that had made him who he was vanished. The body that was strong, supple and invincible in its youth is now ice-cold and, to be honest, problematic. Now it is necessary to bring him away, to his home, if in fact the dead, or their bodies, have some sort of home. Death changes everything. Selfishness was something no-one could connect with Bárður while he lived with such brown eyes, but now his body lies on a baiting table and expects to be cared for, expects to be carried here or there, and besides that seems to blame his former shipmates and Andrea for living.

They eat in silence up in the loft. Almost restlessly. As if they were committing a crime, and they eat less than the sizes of their stomachs demand.

The boy doesn't touch his box, doesn't look at the coffee, he sits on the bed, his and Bárður's bed, a narrow bed that has become uncomfortably wide and far too long, he sits there alone with his waterproof and the book. Then Andrea sits down next to him. Simply sits and stares. The other four finish their bread, finish their coffee, even Einar tries to slurp as little as possible and doesn't complain even though his jaw hurts like hell from the blow. Gvendur has little appetite for his bread, he forces half of it down, then puts it aside as if it were filthy. Pétur stands up, the other three also stand up immediately and go down, Einar grabs Gvendur's slice of bread as he goes down. Pétur pauses, looks at the boy and wants to say something, something about Bárður, something good about Bárður, and then to ask the boy to come down, ask, not order, but they need to work the catch, decapitate, gut, open, flatten, salt, and the boy has his own job in this, he decapitates and guts, cuts the livers out and puts them in barrels, the work is good, it cures all illness. But Pétur is prevented from saying this about the work, that it helps, that we're nothing without it, because Andrea looks at him and her glance says, let him be and go down. And Pétur goes down, with an unexpected lump in his throat. I am losing her, he thinks, no, doesn't think it, feels it, senses it, because between people lie invisible threads and we feel it when they break. They go out to work the catch. Everyone's catch except for Einar's, his line is in the sea, his fish hang on hooks several metres below the storm and do not remember life any differently. Einar is unhappy, it's unfair that he gets nothing while the others get theirs, even Bárður who no longer has any need for it, dead fish for a dead man. They walk out, past the baiting table and the body that once answered to the name of Bárður.

Between those who go to do their duty, their work, to secure their sustenance, and those who sit up in the loft lies a dead man, frozen to death, his eyes are open but have lost their colour and look at nothing. A dead body is useless, we can just as well bin it. The boy looks away, the trapdoor is up, it opens down to death. Hell is a dead person. He moves his right hand to one side, strokes the book that made Bárður forget his waterproof. It is perilous to read poems. The book was printed in Copenhagen in 1828, an epic poem that Reverend Jón translated, reworded, put fifteen years of his life into, an epic composed in England by a blind poet, composed to come closer to God, who is, however, like the sky, the rainbow and the core, he avoids us even as we seek him out.

Paradise Lost.

Is it a loss of Paradise to die?

Andrea thinks about the smell of Bárður's body. That obtrusive blend of warmth and scent. She puts her hand behind her, moves it carefully, and her palm strokes the place where Bárður's head rested in the night. The boy just sits numbly. Once there was a woman who wrote a letter about the moon, once there was a little girl who was proud of having older brothers, once there was a man to whom it was possible to tell everything and he told everything in return, and now they're all dead, except for the moon, and that is just a clod in space, of stone-dead rock and meteorites that have shattered on its surface.

Could it be that a woman's feelings lie higher and thus closer to the skin than a man's? That because a woman can bear life she is in some way more sensitive to it, and to the pain that is only possible to measure in tears, regret, sorrow?

Andrea moves her hand from the end of the bed where Bárður's head lay and places it on the boy's right shoulder. She does this without thinking. This is a movement that comes from within, sympathy and sorrow come together in one hand, and shortly afterwards the boy cries. The tears stream forth when the words are useless stones. He lies like a conch, half in the bed, half in her lap, which will soon be wet with tears. The tears ease the pain and are good but they are still not good enough. It's not possible to thread the tears together and then let them sink like a glittering rope down into the dark deep and pull up those who died but ought to have lived.

It doesn't take the boy long to gather the things he's going to take with him. Andrea helps him, makes him eat something, packs pieces of salted meat for him, the last bits, they were supposed to go into the soup next Sunday, they'll survive without it, she thinks, and quickly feels hot anger towards those outside who have started to work the catch, almost feels hatred that they should be alive, all four of them. Her apron still dark from the tears, perhaps the spot would never disappear, hopefully not, she thinks. They wrap *Paradise Lost* carefully, this book shall be taken along, then enough flatbread and pâté, a handful of sugar cubes. First, however, the boy opens the book and his face twitches when he sees the letter to Sigríður. Nothing is sweet to me, without thee. Words to her who breathes behind the mountains and heaths, and still doesn't know that the possibilities of life have decreased significantly, she who is startled every time she sees someone heading towards the farm and hopes it is the fishing-station postman with a letter for her, a word to bridge distances, words that ease regret, magnify it at the same time and feed it. The next letter she receives will be bulky, passionate words from a dead man. The boy hands Andrea the letter and says, see to it that it goes with him, and Andrea says, poor girl, and that is also what we say, because the frost and the poem took the most precious thing from her.

Then the boy is ready to go.

Of course you're going, Andrea had said, because he couldn't think of lying back down to sleep in the bed without Bárður there, of sitting down on the thwart without Bárður there. Bárður is gone and a frozen body is all that's left. It would be a betrayal, the boy had said, I couldn't bear it.

Two explanations, two excuses, everything has at least two sides.

They hurry because Pétur isn't going to take this well, a man doesn't leave his crew, that's simply absurd, I'll deal with Pétur, Andrea says, just go, you don't belong here, and the boy goes where he and Bárður had headed in the spring, here to the Village, the centre, the hub of the world.

Be careful on that damned Impassable, no doubt the waves are breaking well over it by now, Andrea says, and the boy says, yes, I'll be careful, but doesn't say that he plans to take a different route, through the valley that cleaves between the mountains, he's going up onto the heath and then the plateau, wants to come as far from the sea as possible, though it might only be for one night or two, it's a long way and dangerous in such weather, at this time of year, but what does it matter since most of them are dead, who cares whether I live, thinks the boy, but he says nothing, promises to take care about the surf, Andrea would never let him go if she knew the route he was planning to take. And what then, she asks. I'll return the book, he says simply. She strokes his face with both hands, she kisses his forehead, she kisses both his eyebrows, don't forget me, boy, she says, never, he says, and vanishes into the snowdrift.

VI

Those who live in this valley see only a piece of the sky. Their horizon is mountains and dreams.

The boy knows this valley, and knows that whoever follows it and then threads his way along a particular path between the mountainsides cut by ravines and crosses two plateaus comes down into the valley that Bárður had called his district and one farm in the valley his home. The boy doesn't head towards home, how is it possible to head towards a place that doesn't exist, not even in our heads? He doesn't call the valley his district, although he'd slept and awakened there for most of his life, and no farm his home. Some need to live a long time to have the place that releases these big words, *at home*, from the fetters of language, and more and more die without having found it. He intends never to return to the district that contains the better part of his youth, the dreams that never came true and the regret for the life he never got to live, that contains the people he had lived with since his father drowned and came into possession of his dark abode in the sea, the people he grew up with, fell asleep apart from and woke up among, not bad people, no, no, but he simply never got rid of the feeling that the farm and the valley were little more than stopping places for the night. One needs a place to sit down for a moment, linger while the body grows and the mind becomes large enough to deal with the world on its own. Otherwise it's a beautiful district, unusually grassy and spacious, a considerable stretch to the sea from several farms and from the doorsteps of some of them not even a glimpse of it, which is unusual here, how is it possible to live without having the sea before one's eyes? The sea is the wellspring of life, in it dwells the rhythm of death, and now the boy heads away from this, as far away as he can get, even if only for one night or two, just come so far that he no longer senses the sea.

He trudges into the valley and Bárður is dead.

Read a poem and froze to death because of it.

Some poems take us places where no words reach, no thought, they take you up to the core itself, life stops for one moment and becomes beautiful, it becomes clear with regret and happiness. Some poems change the day, the night, your life. Some poems make you forget, forget the sadness, the hopelessness, you forget your waterproof, the frost comes to you, says, got you, and you're dead. The one who dies is changed immediately into the past. It doesn't matter how important a person was, how much kindness and strength of will that person had and how life was inconceivable without him or her: death says, got you, life vanishes in a second and the person is changed into the past. Everything connected to that person becomes a memory you struggle to retain, and it is treachery to forget that. Forget how he drank coffee. Forget how he laughed. How he looked up. But still you forget. Life demands that you do. You forget slowly but surely, and it can be so painful that it pierces the heart.

It's an effort to wade through the snow.

The boy walks straight ahead, thinks that he does.

He walks and walks and walks, the snowfall is dense and swirling, visibility only a few metres, he stops once to eat, then starts walking again and it starts to grow dim, he sees and senses how the daylight is dwindling between snowflakes, how the wind is darkening. The only sensible thing to do would be to find a farm and ask for shelter, but he trudges on, caring not a whit for sensibility, only half caring whether he survives the night or not. Yet. He has this book on his back, *Paradise Lost*, and one should return one's books. It's likely the reason why Andrea ordered him to take the book with him, she knows him and this peculiar love of his for books. The boy suddenly feels warm inside when he thinks about Andrea, but the warmth cools quickly because Bárður froze to death, and right next to him. It's also dark, from the evening, the dense snowfall and the gathering drifts.

As a matter of fact the visibility does not decrease significantly with the onset of evening, yet darkness is always darkness, and evening is always evening. And the evening becomes night that settles on the eyes, sifts its way through the cornea, fills the optic nerve; slowly but surely this walking boy is filled with night. He wants most to lie down, just where he's standing, relieve himself of his burden, lie down on his back with his eyes open, the world darkens except for the snowflakes nearest to him, they are white, cut like angels' wings. The snow would cover him, he would die into the whiteness. It's very tempting, the boy says to himself, out loud or silently, he has long since stopped making the distinction; whoever walks for a long time and alone in a ceaseless snowfall comes little by little to the feeling that he has left the world, walks in no-man's land, the surety of life leaves him. Then it stops snowing. It sounds incredible, but it always stops snowing in the end, and then he stands perhaps in front of a farm, the storm and the night had completely cut all human ties. Very tempting, the boy says to himself, to stop this tiring hike, lie down, sleep, yes, and then die. Of course it would be good to die, no more trouble, sorrow conquered, regret conquered. It's also so short between life and death, actually just one piece of clothing, one waterproof.

First there's life, then there's death:

I live, she lives, they live, he dies.

But if I die here, then the book I'm supposed to return will be damaged and I would disappoint some people, the old sea captain, whom I otherwise couldn't care less about, Andrea and Bárður. Bárður is of course dead but not his presence: it has never been stronger. Yes, first I return the book, then I can walk off into the wilderness and the snow can cover me, thinks the boy, but he knows that then he will have to choose the place for this carefully. It's easy to let oneself be covered with snow, easy to die, but let's not forget that the night and the snowfall deceive, the boy thinks he lies down far from all human habitation, in the wilderness, but is then perhaps on a slope above a little farm, the snow melts after days or weeks, he appears dead beneath it, and a little girl or little boy comes across the corpse damaged by weather and insects, both eyes taken by the ravens, empty, dark holes, and he or she will never get over seeing such a thing. Dying has its responsibilities. Dammit, then I'll go on, thinks the boy, disappointed, or says it out loud, and trudges forward, wades through the snow, senses with his feet whether the land is rising or falling, turns away from the slope and tries thereby to keep himself more or less in the middle of the valley. But the night becomes heavier and the snow becomes ever more difficult to cross, until finally he has no idea whether he is heading up or down, but still he walks southwards, this he feels from the wind that presses constantly on his back, at some point however he needs to turn east to make it up to the heath and then the plateau. This is just so difficult. His feet have started to whimper with fatigue, best to rest. The boy feels his way forward, searching for a crag or rock large enough to shelter him from the northerly, which is cold and would have no trouble turning him to ice. He finds shelter, starts to pack the snow around him, keeps on until he has made a kind of wall and partial roof, in fact it's more of a snow-hole than a house, but he is no longer out in the wind and the snowfall and he is so tired. His fatigue is enormously heavy. It fills every cell, every thought. Probably twenty-four hours since he opened his eyes, since he woke to Pétur's voice and into the world in which Bárður was alive, how many years ago was it actually, he thinks, and the wind blows outside. The boy's face is stiff from the cold, the ice covering his sweater starts to thaw, he's drenched and his face is wet, difficult to say whether he cries in his sleep or while awake, there isn't always shelter in dreams, sometimes not at all. But be careful, boy, not to sleep too long or too soundly, because whoever sleeps soundly in such a snow-hole, in such dark weather, never wakes again in this life. Then spring comes and a little girl goes to pick flowers above her farm but finds you and you're no flower, you're just a rotting body and the source of nightmares.

Hell Is
Not Knowing Whether We Are
Alive or Dead

Hell is not knowing whether we are alive or dead.

I live, she lives, they live, he dies.

This rough conjugation struck us like a mace on the head, because the story about the boy, the snow, the huts, almost made us forget our own deaths. We are no longer alive: the Unnameable is between us and you. The region that no-one has crossed by any other means than losing their lives, and there is likely no greater loss. Yet there exist, as you know, countless stories about the dead crossing the Immeasurable and manifesting themselves among the living, yet they appear never to have brought any important messages, never told any great news of eternal life, and how does that happen?

To die is the pure white movement, says one poem.

It shall be admitted that we feared death until the last moment of life and fought against it as long as we could endure it, until something came and extinguished the lights, but mixed with the fear was curiosity, a hesitant, fearful inquisitiveness, because now all of the questions would be answered. Then we died and nothing happened. Our eyes closed and we opened them again in precisely the same place, we saw everything but no-one saw us, we were in bodies and yet bodiless, we had voices and yet were voiceless. Weeks passed, months, years passed, and those who continued to live grew away from us and then died, we don't know where they went. Ten years, twenty years, thirty years, forty, fifty, sixty, seventy, how long do we need to count, how high is it possible to reach? Here we are, above ground, restless, terrified and embittered, while our bones are likely peaceful down in the ground, with our names on crosses above them. The tedium can be total, even universal, and we would long ago have lost our minds if only we could have done. The only thing we can do, apart from following along with you and others who live, is to ask constantly, why are we here? Where did the others go? What can ease the sting? Where is God? We ask and ask but it seems there are no answers, it is likely just priests, politicians and advertisers who have them at the ready.

There is sometimes so much tranquillity here that our heartbeats are the only thing to be heard, which is simply deplorable; we die, close our eyes and disappear to everything that matters, then open our eyes again and the heart still beats, the only organ that knows its job. Purpose, is that the blue sky we never touch? We roam around here and there is something invisible between us and you who live, we walk through walls, both ironbound and old wooden walls, we loiter in parlours and gape with you at the television, look over your shoulders when you read the papers, when you read a book. We sit entire nights in the churchyard with our backs against headstones, our legs drawn up to our chests and our hands around our knees, like Bárður when he felt the frost creep close to his heart. Occasionally a feeble sound carries to us in the still of the night, simple, half-broken notes that seem to come from a great distance. This is God, we then say hopefully, this is the sound that is heard when God comes and fetches those who have waited long enough and never doubted. This is what we say and we are optimistic, not entirely dismayed yet. But maybe this is not God, maybe someone is simply lying in the ground with a little music box, turning the handle when he's bored.

Hell is to be dead and to realize that you did not care for life while you had the chance to do so. A person, by the way, is a remarkable creation, living as well as dead. When it winds up in trouble, if its existence is cut in two, it starts involuntarily to review its life, it seeks its memories like a little animal seeking shelter in its hole. And that's how it is with us. It's something of a relief to follow along with your life, a comfort that yet becomes bitter when you treat your life badly, do something that will torment you eternally, but it is first and last our own memories that we try to reach, they are the thread that connects us to life. Memories of the days when we so truly lived, when it snowed and rained over our lives and the hours were warm with sun, dark with night.

But why tell you these stories?

What terrifying powers, other than despair, fling us over the Unnameable in order to tell you stories of extinguished lives?

Our words are confused rescue teams with obsolete maps and birdsong in place of compasses. Confused and profoundly lost, yet their job is to save the world, save extinguished lives, save you and then hopefully us as well. But we will put off further reflections and weighty questions and return once more to the night and the storm, find the boy and try to save him in time from sleep and death.

The Boy, the Village
and the Profane Trinity

I

The boy did not fall asleep in the snow-hole. All the same, sleep offered to take him in its downy-soft arms, to ease the fatigue that was so heavy that each of his eyelids weighed at least half a kilogram, sleep was actually an offer he could not refuse, but he tore himself away from its succour, tried to keep himself awake by thinking of Bárður, because sorrow has deprived so many of sleep. He also thought about Andrea, who had allowed him to set out into this snowstorm, or rather, in into it. If he fell asleep here in this hole, if he gave in to the soothing voice of sleep, he would not reawaken, at least not in this life.

It was thus conscientiousness that kept sleep and death from the boy. He needed to return a book, he could not let down Andrea, could not let down Bárður, his memory, could not let down his mother and his sister who never got to grow up and died before her childish admiration for her brothers behind the mountain managed to fade, to fall asleep here would be to let them all down, and thus he pulled himself up from the hole.

Stood up quickly and was once again in the dense snowfall,

the night and the frost-hardened world.

He gasped for breath because of the storm and started off.

He hikes up from the valley. Up onto the heath and the plateau into which it turns, barren and nearly level: the glacier planed off the top of the mountain ages ago. The boy has the arctic wind mostly at his back and the night surrounds him, it is within the snowfall, within the white snowflakes. The boy has never before come so high, never made it so close to the sky and at the same time never been as far from it. He inches forward, abandoned by all but God, and there is no God. It's so cold. His head is frozen and his brain has changed into an expansive tundra, hoar-frosted and frozen earth as far as the eye can see, completely lifeless on the surface, but underneath are hidden weak embers, memories, faces, sentences, nothing is sweet to me, without thee. These embers could conceivably melt the hoar frost, call to birds, waken the fragrance of blossoms. But up here on the plateau nothing is fragrant, there are just the frost and the night, he walks on, time passes, morning comes. And the morning passes as well. He no longer sustains a thought, his feet keep going like a machine, which is very good, yet he must be careful because everything ends, even plateaus, and in some places they end abruptly, simply cease to exist, and the dizzying fall begins.

It is actually amazing that he did not walk off the edge and plunge to his death. As indifferent as he was, giddy from the frost, fatigue, numbed by sorrow. But perhaps he senses a slight change long gone and with the expansive tundra in his head, stiff extremities and a terribly heavy burden on his back, a book that killed his best, no, his one friend. It was such a short time since they had walked together out of the Village, side by side, the boy whimpers a bit as he walks, although he scarcely has the energy to do so, it is afternoon and the snow has stopped falling from the sky. The boy walks along the beach wherever possible, otherwise on the tussocky moorland that lies between the mountains and the beach, several dozen metres wide at best. He stops at a little river and regards the iron pipe that Friðrik, the Factor at Tryggvi's Shop, the Village's largest shop, had installed in it; a long pipe and a large trestle, half-buried in the ground, under one of its ends, the water runs pure and clear there and never freezes. Friðrik's men row daily across the Lagoon to fetch water for the shop and the boats when they're ready to go. Of course the Village does not lack wells, but the water in them is not particularly good, blended with seawater and sometimes filth, some people think it's fun to throw rubbish into the wells and even to piss in them, some people are so strange it's as if the Devil has bitten them in the ass. The boy gulps down ice-cold water. He looks out over the Lagoon and at the old Danish trading houses on the Point, the oldest buildings in the Village, from the early eighteenth century. Two storehouses, now used for the same purpose by Tryggvi's Shop, and the Factor's house, which has been used in recent years as the residence of the the shop's head assistant. The house is very haunted; the assistant and his wife are the only ones who have stayed there for more than

one year, some say it's only because the couple lack the imagination to perceive the haunting. The boy squints to see the buildings
better, they are dark, it's as though the air is hazy, it's bright
enough but difficult to see fine details from a distance. He resumes
walking. The water has done him good, given him the strength to
move his feet, and it's also good not to have to wade through the
snow, the beach is empty and quite easy to traverse, not covered
with large rocks and uneven as it is around the fishing station,
where it is shaped by the vehemence of the ocean. Then he recalls
how it was only forty-eight hours ago that they sat together on
the bed, read and waited for Árni. He is so overcome that he
walks up the mountainside, sits down between two large rocks
and stares out with empty eyes while the afternoon air grows
heavier and turns into evening around him.

Why go on?

And what is he doing here?

Shouldn't he have stayed on at the fishing station, to keep an
eye on the dead body and then bring it to its home, what were
friends for, and shouldn't friendship overcome the grave and
death? He sighs because he has betrayed everything. He sits there
for a long time and it starts to snow again. Would it snow over the
valley where so many people think about Bárður, or is there a
moon in the sky, wading in clouds, and has Bárður's betrothed
come out to gaze at it? Bárður always went out at 8.00 to gaze at
the moon and at the same time she stood outside the farmhouse
and watched as well, there were mountains and distances between

them but their eyes met on the moon, precisely as the eyes of lovers have done since the beginning of time, and that is why the moon was placed in the sky.

The boy has started walking again. He threads his way along the beach until he comes to the church, where he has to turn and wade through the snow again. He leans for a moment against the churchyard wall and looks out into the snowfall that hides the Village, catches a faint glimpse of the houses next to the church, dim lights in one or two windows, many people having presumably gone to bed, but not sleeping as soundly as those behind him. He can still make out the path of the priest, Reverend Þorvaldur, from the church and down to his street. The boy threads the path, it makes the going easier, but not by much. The street where the Café is located is covered with snow, and Þorvaldur's path dwindles there and disappears. The boy stands in the middle of the street, snow falls on him, his left foot weighs a hundred kilograms, his right foot three hundred, and there is far too much snow between him and the Café. He could just stand there in the same place until morning in the hope that Lúlli and Oddur would come along here to cut a path with their shovels, but that isn't what he does, doesn't know that Lúlli and Oddur exist, even less that they work in the winters shovelling the streets of the Village, so incredibly lucky to have steady jobs from September until May, goddamn dogs, why does luck stick to some and not others? There are eight houses on the street, all stately. The boy wades through snowdrifts and approaches the houses and Geirþrúður's café. The

104

life he has lived until now is past, before him is utter uncertainty, and the only certain thing is that he plans to return the book and report the news of Bárður's death, announce that the only thing that mattered is gone and will never return. Then why continue to live, why, he mumbles to the snowflakes, which do not reply, they are just white and fall silently to the ground. Now I'll go in and return the book, thanks for the loan, this is magnificent writing, nothing is sweet to me, without thee, it killed my best friend, the only good thing that was possible to find in this damned life, that is to say, thanks for the loan, and then he would say goodbye, or no, forget that, just turn on his heel and walk back out, struggle down to the hotel, the World's End Hotel, take a basement room, pay later or, in other words, never, because tomorrow or tomorrow evening he is going to kill himself. This suddenly comes to him, the solution appears, just like that. Kill himself, then all the uncertainty is behind him. He thought of thanking God, but something held him back. Bárður had told him about Suicide Cliff: he would go there, easy as air to walk off it, the sea would take care of the rest, it knows how to drown people, is highly trained, the boy would go immediately if he weren't so damned tired and horribly hungry, and then he also needs to return a book. He wades through the final metres of snow, slowly, with difficulty.

No-one is out and about in the entire Village except for this boy, who is too tired and hungry to die.

II

How many years fit into one day, one day and one night? It is a middle-aged man, not a nineteen-year-old boy, who opens the outer door to Geirþrúður's café more than forty-eight hours after he walked through the same door for the first time with his friend Bárður, the boy misses him so much that he needs to rest his forehead for a long time on the wall inside the entrance, or whatever we ought to call this little space where Jens the overland postman usually keeps his boxes and bags until Dr Sigurður fetches them, or sends someone after them, while Jens forgets the difficulties of life by drinking beer. The boy stares into the wall for a long time with wide-open eyes, then looks down at several pairs of shoes made of sea-wolf skin. Guests are expected to take off their boots here, if they're covered in filth and mud, and slip on these fish-skin shoes instead. Many people find this an unnecessary ostentation, no doubt extreme, and some people stubbornly resist but have to give in if they wish to be served, and who doesn't remove his footwear if there's hope of a beer? I'm not taking off anything, the boy says quietly to himself, but, on the other hand, he needs to open another door to go all the way inside, the inner door opens into the Café itself, thus ensuring that the cold from outside does not follow guests in unhindered, life is a struggle to hold the cold at bay. Thirty years, mutters the boy, thirty years since I was here with Bárður. He looks at the door, so that's how it looks, and that's how the door handle is, remarkable, he thinks, but then everything becomes hazy, tears appear in the corners of his eyes and they muddle his sight. The boy doesn't cry for long, several tears, several small boats that run down his cheeks heavily laden with sorrow.

The boy takes a deep breath, opens the door and is startled by the jingling of the bell above it.

He immediately sees three men in the corner farthest from him, of course he sees them, there are no others here, just these men and eight to ten empty tables. The men look up, they all look at him, then the thing occurs that he finds so unbearable and that he despises himself for: his shyness sweeps sorrow and grief from him, deprives him of thought, he becomes nothing but nervousness, uncertainty, and he has no idea what he ought to do. The only thing that comes into his mind is to sit down, which he does, sits down at the table as far from the men as possible, turns sideways to them and sits straight-backed, white with snow. It's dim inside, two paraffin lamps glow on the walls and a candle on the table of the three men, a heavy chandelier hangs above the centre of the room. He had been transfixed by it on his previous visit, but now he simply stares at nothing and then the snow starts to melt off him. He looks out the window as if he has walked for thirty-six hours in storm and darkness for the one purpose of sitting down and looking out the window. In that case he would have enough to keep him occupied for the next several hours, there are six windows in the Café and all of them dimly reflect the light within, dim mirrors. The boy sees little of the evening that fills the world outside, more of the idiot sitting there by himself at his table, the snow melting off him. I'm such a small character that I'll more than likely melt with the snow, change into a puddle that dries up, change into a dark spot that then disappears. He looks at himself in the window with disgust, punishes himself by looking, but finally looks down at the tabletop, so the tabletop's like that, one can easily spend one's time looking at a tabletop, but if he makes an effort he can catch a glimpse of the three men, recognizes Kolbeinn and his blind eyes, grumpy as a sea-wolf, Bárður had said with a grin, yet liked him very much. The boy finds it highly unlikely that he will ever be like Kolbeinn. In the first place he's malicious as hell, in the second place a dirty dog, and in the third place I'll be dead tomorrow. But he has a lot of books, real books at that, not rhymes and ballads, Bibles and hymns and sermons and things like that, but poetry, instructional books, why does a bad man have so many books, books should make men good, thinks the boy.

He's so naïve.

The men have started talking together, probably to make fun of him, but the boy unfortunately doesn't understand a word of what they're saying, it's actually just completely unintelligible noises coming from them. At first he listens in surprise but finally realizes that this must be Cod language, very strange that he's never heard it before. He raises his head slightly and glances over, no longer needs to roll his eyes as if he were being strangled. Has never seen the other two, both big men and undoubtedly fishermen, from a ship, he thinks, otherwise they would be at a fishing station, I hope the Devil takes them tonight and shoves red-hot pokers deep up their asses. Refreshing to think like that, refreshing to be bad, one isn't being shy when one is being bad, he's no longer a wretch melting with the snow. Now he sits and simply stares at nothing and couldn't care less about anything or anyone. Wonder if their dialect is called Coddish? Then he notices that the snow is melting quickly and a large puddle has formed on the floor. Dammit. Should've brushed myself off at the door. Bloody hell. This Helga can't stand folk bringing dirt and water in with them. I wouldn't want to mess with her! Bárður had said, damn me if I'm not sometimes half afraid of her.

If Bárður was afraid of this woman, then I'll probably be terrified, thinks the boy in his wet seat.

The men laugh Coddishly, and of course at him. It must be useful for fishermen to understand Coddish, it would be enough for them to stick their heads into the sea, shout something and their boats would be filled. What is *death* in Coddish? Probably *omaúnu*, and that with a capital O: *Omaúnu*. It hurts his eyes to look sideways so intensely. The other two are perhaps old shipmates of

Kolbeinn and have started to grow old like him, one broad-shouldered, bald and with terrifically large eyebrows, the other with short grey hair and a strikingly large potato-nose, it would fill the palm of a medium-sized man, both are fully bearded, unkempt beards that reach down to their chests, making them appear even bigger. Maybe I should grow a beard, thinks the boy, it would take me just under a month to cover my cheeks, but then he remembers that he had thought of dying tomorrow and completely gives up on the idea of growing a beard. Suddenly he is standing up. It happens almost without his realizing it. Stands between the tables, perplexed. They stop talking and look at him, except for Kolbeinn, the blind one, who sticks out his chin and cocks his left ear towards him as if it were a malformed eye. Bottles of Carlsberg beer in front of them on the table, one of them nearly full. The boy takes three steps, reaches for a bottle, pours the beer down his throat and then sees Helga, who is standing next to the counter, staring at him. Incredible what a big man he suddenly was. The boy turns on his heel, opens his bag, pulls out the book, unwraps it and holds it up, holds onto it as if it were a declaration, or a symbol, and says to Kolbeinn, Bárður asked me to convey his gratitude for the loan.

The old sea-wolf doesn't react. No more than the other three. They just watch and appear to be waiting for him to say something else.

But there's some kind of damned veil over the boy's head that causes him not to be completely sure of when he is thinking and when he is speaking. Maybe he didn't say anything just now, simply held the book above his head and said nothing. Because of this he clears his throat forcefully, takes a deep breath and applies all his might to deliver this message:

> BÁRÐUR ASKED ME TO CONVEY HIS GRATITUDE
> FOR THE LOAN.
> HE WOULD REALLY HAVE LIKED TO HAVE
> READ FURTHER IN IT AND LEARN MORE LINES
> BY HEART, BUT HE CAN'T DO THAT NOW
> UNFORTUNATELY, THAT IS TO SAY HE FORGOT
> HIS WATERPROOF AND FROZE TO DEATH, WE
> LAID HIM OUT ON THE BAITING TABLE AND
> THERE HE LAY WHEN I SAW HIM LAST.
> THANK YOU VERY MUCH.

He concludes his speech abruptly, lays the book carefully on the table next to the three men, bends to retrieve his mittens, shoves his hands into them, what was I thanking them for, he thinks, I'm always the same damned fool, throws his bag over his shoulder and goes to the door but no further, he feels a heavy weight on his left shoulder, a hand or the sky, he collapses, his feet give way, it's simply like that, they are no longer standing beneath him and he collapses to the floor and lies there in a heap. Unconsciousness comes and collects him.

III

Around eight hundred people live here in the Village.

There is much that fits into eight hundred souls.

Many worlds, many dreams. A swarm of events, heroism and cowardice, betrayal and devotion, good times and bad.

Some live in such a way that it is noticed and their existence sets something in the air in motion, others hang on to life for many years, even eighty, but never touch anything, time goes through them and then they are dead, buried, forgotten. Live for eighty years but still do not live, one might even mention a betrayal of life, because there are others who are born and die before they manage to say their first word, get a stomach ache, a bad cold, and Jón the joiner needs to make a little coffin, a little box to go around a life that never was, except for a few sleepless nights, irresistible eyes, such small toes that they resembled a miracle. Paid a short visit like the dew. Gone when we awoke and the only thing we can do is hope deep inside, where the heart beats and dreams dwell, that no life is wasted, is without purpose.

*

Numbers have no imagination and therefore you can't make much of them. According to maps the mountains here rise nine hundred metres into the sky, which is absolutely correct, some days they do that, but one morning when we wake and look out the mountains have grown considerably taller and are at least three thousand metres, they scratch the sky and our hearts shrink. On those days it is difficult to stoop over salt fish on the drying lot. The mountains are not a part of the landscape, they are the landscape.

The sand Spit on which the Village stands stretches out like a bent arm into the slender fjord and reaches nearly across it. The sea within the arm of the Spit is sheltered and freezes readily, changes into smooth ice, we whistle at the moon and emerge from our houses with ice skates. It is often placid here because these mountains stop the winds, yet you shouldn't think there is eternal calm in our village and that feathers lost by flying angels float down to us, of course this happens but make no mistake, a gale can certainly blow in! The mountains deepen the calm and they also magnify the winds, which can rush wildly into the fjord, arctic winds full of murderous intent, and everything that is not securely fastened blows away and disappears. Beams, shovels, carts, roof tiles, entire roofs, right-footed boots, ideals, lukewarm expressions of love. The wind howls between the mountains, tears up the sea, the saltiness settles on the houses and cellars flood. When it becomes calm and we can go outside without dying, the streets are covered with seaweed, as if the sea has sneezed over us. But the calm always returns, angel feathers float down, we stand on the

V

Geirþrúður is not from here. No-one seems to know for sure where she came from, where she grew up. She appears here one day with old Guðjón, wealthy Guðjón. Thirty years younger than him, even thirty-five, with her pitch-black hair, tall, eyes darklike pieces of coal, a few dull freckles across her nose gave her an appearance of innocence and it was no doubt because of this, some would suggest, that the old man fell for her, as tired of life as he had become, you should never trust freckles. On the other hand we know Guðjón well, or knew him, born and raised here, descended from wealthy landowners, started a fishing company, bought shares in the Norwegian whaling station on the next fjord and made so much money that even the big merchants, Leó and Tryggvi, had no control over him, yet they control everything they care to control, what houses are built, what roads laid, who receives maintenance from the parish, who goes to Hell and who to Heaven. Guðjón's wealth was of course not as magnificent as theirs, they were Germany and Britain, he perhaps Sweden, the rest of us scarcely a parish in Iceland. Guðjón married rather young.

That's common here. We marry young so we can lie close together when darkness and cold rule the world. His wife was descended from fine burgesses, willowy, with mousy hair, prone to laughter, and him this huge body, more than medium height, sturdy, and early on became quite stout and rather excitable, he'll crush the girl, we said, yet she wasn't crushed, Guðjón must have been careful, they had three children, lived together for almost thirty years and then she died. There was a piano in their home, heavy furniture, a carpet, a portrait of Jón Sigurðsson, and Dr Sigurður lived a short distance away, but she died all the same. Guðjón never got over her death, the foundations of his life cracked, he started to drink copiously and he and the priest did various untoward things when the nights were longest, but his boys went to study at the Learned School and one of them all the way to Copenhagen, settled down there in some sort of business, the other is an official in Reykjavík and is under the Governor's wing, they never come here. The daughter of course learned to play the piano, to sew, how to curtsey and make conversation at banquets, learned three languages, was encouraged to read long novels, she played Chopin and a Norwegian whaling captain heard her playing through the open window, she moved to Norway the year after and we haven't seen her since. Old Guðjón remained behind alone. Restless, unhappy, bloated from sleeplessness and drinking, bought himself a pistol from an English sea captain, placed it against his temple thrice in as many years but didn't have the strength to pull the trigger and break into the realm of death.

least until one of them came up with the idea of opening the window onto the autumn and the sky coughed when the smoke was sucked out. Guðjón looked at the glowing embers of the cigarette, I asked, he said, what she wanted to do in this life, there must have been something she wanted to experience. To eat breakfast in an old German village in the mountains, she replied. And that's what we did. That's why we travelled around Germany, ate breakfast in a village in the mountains, married in the afternoon in a three-hundred-year-old mountain chapel. She just wants everything you own, old friend, said Lárus sadly and angrily, you're humiliating yourself, added Þorvaldur and clenched his fists instinctively, but then Guðjón smirked: you're just jealous of my getting to sleep with a young woman, so young, beautiful and so white-skinned, besides which she's smarter than I am and s ays things that get me to look at the world differently. You could surely have managed to sleep with her without marrying her and then dragging her out here, what do you know, maybe people are laughing at you, what do you know, maybe she's waiting to get rid of you, take it all and leave? Guðjón looked directly into Lárus' face with the blue eyes that could become oddly sad, as in an old dog, but could also be piercing and terrifying. Lárus looked away, was going to apologize, but then Guðjón cleared his throat, spit into the spittoon and said, life was pointless for us both, so it was logical to marry, our age difference matters little.

They lived their first year in his old house, which stands on Main Street. A beautiful house in an excellent location, but the rectory. There is a carpet on the floor, a heavy chandelier in the parlour, the piano that Guðjón sometimes hammered on in his despair and called it playing. Þorvaldur was happy having his friend next door, it is so unbelievably good to have a friend in this world, then you aren't quite as defenceless, you can talk to someone and listen without needing to guard your heart at the same time. The winter evenings are also long here, they string darkness from one mountaintop to another, the children fall asleep and then the racket falls silent, we get time to read, think. But when the children fall asleep innocence retreats and we perhaps remember death, the solitude, then it's a blessing to have a friend next door and endlessly good to hold a cigar in the office or Guðjón's study, see the embers glow, watch as they burn slowly upwards. Þorvaldur and Guðjón could sit like that for hours at a time. Talk about the government, about the Danes, about fishing, whether using shellfish for bait should or should not be banned, whether the Village should invest in a steamship, they spoke about municipal concerns. It was a great relief for Guðjón to talk about the problems of the world out there, where the issues are clear and the words don't disturb the heart, don't touch the wound deep inside us. Good evening for both of them, a good diversion and happy steps from the rectory to Guðjón's Norwegian house, a happy twenty-eight steps, but Þorvaldur was always just as uncertain regarding Geirþrúður. She was courteous, no doubt about that, came with refreshments, smiled at him, asked questions that were easy to answer, but he always had the feeling that something was lurking beneath the surface, perhaps scorn, or just disrespect, and he disapproved of how little gratitude she, this former chambermaid in a Reykjavík hotel, displayed at having been raised so unexpectedly into the ranks of better society. She was, for example, soon invited, as the wife of wealthy Guðjón, to join the Eve women's club, twenty or thirty women who meet regularly and chat about life and the world, about shortages and adultery. They sponsor the children's Christmas pageant, collect donations when young women lose their husbands to the sea and are left behind alone with large numbers of children, at times get learned men to lecture to them. Geirþrúður attended twice. Unfortunately I don't feel like sitting entire evenings over sweets and listening to women talk about obvious things, she explained to Guðrún when the priest's wife came to visit and asked why Geirþrúður had stopped coming. You're perhaps superior to us, Guðrún said, coldly courteous.

Why should I be?

Guðrún looked silently for a long time at Geirþrúður, who looked back at her quizzically, even innocently. We invited you out of goodwill, it was out of goodwill that I came here, and goodwill is not small change you find in the street.

I'm not one for company, the younger woman interjected.

Are you asking me to leave?

No, I'm just not one for company.

You're not particularly friendly, I must say.

It's not my intention to be unfriendly, I'm just trying to be honest.

They sat in the elegant parlour, which later was turned into the Café, the thick carpet dampened all sound, a large, old grandfather clock ticked away in a corner, otherwise there was silence. Guðrún looked down into the blue-white porcelain cup half full of tea, Geirþrúður drank coffee from a large cup, Helga came in with more coffee, Geirþrúður drank it like water. Guðrún waited until Helga had gone out again, this silent housekeeper whom Geirþrúður had sent for from Reykjavík, just as grumpy and unsociable as the housewife herself, aren't you even grateful, Guðrún asked, after the door had closed behind Helga and they were left alone with the time in the spacious parlour. For what, the other woman asked, seemingly surprised.

Do I need to spell it out?

Yes, you most likely do, unfortunately.

Very good, Guðrún said, and she straightened herself in her seat, sat up and looked hard at the young woman, we know this look, it penetrates walls, Þorvaldur fears it more than almost anything else. Do you think, she said, speaking slowly, that it's completely natural for a man like Guðjón, who is far from being an ordinary man and in addition is extremely well off financially, to take up with you, make an average girl, a chambermaid, his equal by marrying her? And do you think it's normal and natural for the rest of us to welcome you unconditionally into our group, even treat you with motherly affection and tolerance?

Unfortunately, I'm not average, and unfortunately, I'm not a girl.

Yes, of course you're a girl, Guðrún said sharply, she cannot bear it when people doubt what seems clear to her, you are a girl, average or not, we won't go into that now, who becomes suddenly the wife of a wealthy man but who of course clearly shows signs of being lower-class. I don't say this to criticize you, we are what we are, but with the will and the correct disposition it is possible to learn much, and you should be able to devote yourself to customs and habits that do not perhaps lie completely in your nature, but then you also need to spend time with the right people. A woman of your class does not for example gulp coffee from a crock like a fisherman's wife, like a fisherman, I feel I have to say. A woman of your class sits up straight, not like an unruly child.

Geirþrúður looked down, as if to inspect herself, she sat crosswise in the green, downy-soft, wide chair, one leg over one of the arms, her hands around her coffee cup as if she were cold, she seemed to think things over for a moment and then said, without looking directly at Guðrún, I agreed to marry Guðjón because he's a good man, because we feel happy together and because I view him as my equal.

Guðrún brought the cup calmly to her lips, then set it down empty, you're not Guðjón's equal and you never will be, she said, and she stood up, looked down at Geirþrúður, I expect that you won't be coming to another Eve meeting.

Unfortunately, I have little appetite for sweets.

Or the company of others, the priest's wife added.

Geirþrúður then smiled for the first time and said, we two

could almost get on, yes, Guðrún replied, almost.

She's weaselled her way into the life of a lonely middle-aged man, quite a few people said, she deprived him of the tranquility of his twilight years, and sure enough, one day Guðjón grabbed at his chest, it was right outside on the street and in the sunshine, looked around amazed and then was dead. Geirþrúður inherited half, which was no trifle, and did not shed a single tear at the funeral. However, she spared no expense on the wake, we'll give her that, it was a great wake and as joyful as if the Devil had kindled a fire under the attendees. Þorvaldur became unforgivably drunk and wound up in the wrong bed with a cheerful housemaid, Gunnhildur, who found it both funny and titillating to be with the priest, she made him wear his cassock throughout and it was fun while it lasted, but not after he sobered up, then it was not fun at all, and two days later Þorvaldur had joined the Daybreak Temperance Society. Geirþrúður on the other hand wasn't seen at the wake, she was of course up at the house counting the money, said one man, I thought I saw her walking up above the town, said another, yes, probably to meet the Devil, her husband, said the third, but in any case, many of them woke up terribly hung over, with Guðjón in the ground, waiting for Doomsday. Then Geirþrúður opened the Café where the house's elegant parlour had been, she called it simply The Café, but we have sometimes used such names as The Pub, The Refuge, The Gates of Hell.

VI

The boy still sleeps, heavily, unconsciously. Dreams sometimes free us from life. They are the sunshine behind the world. We lie down to sleep at the end of a January evening, the north wind shakes the house, the thin windowpanes tremble, we close our eyes and the sun shines on us. Those who live beneath falling mountainsides and so close to the end of the world are specialists in dreams. The boy sleeps. Then he wakes up, comes slowly to the surface.

It is still dark when he wakes up.

Feels, however, that the night is behind him and that the sun will soon rise from the deep.

He opens his eyes slowly, cautiously, reluctantly, and the dreams that had filled existence are sundered and turn to nothing, at most a trace of fog that hangs over the memory for a few seconds and then dissipates. He closes his eyes again, awake yet not completely. A cosy condition he has often tried to maintain, precisely in the middle, sleep on the one hand, waking on the other, holding waking at bay as long as he can. Imagined that he was waking up in a house with a piano, a barrel organ, a wall covered in books, people in this house are thoughtful, know a lot and there is even an apple on the table. But reality never lets you stray far from it, you only ever escape it for a moment, the living and the dead are in its hands, thus it's a question of mental and spiritual health, of Hell and Heaven, of making reality a better place. Daydreams retreat, the apple, thinking people, the piano, the books. Then the boy tries to imagine that he's at the fishing station, that he's waking up, the fishing voyage ahead and Bárður alive. He sniffs in the hope of smelling the odour of his friend's sweaty feet but the air in the room is far too good, not deadly close as it is after sleeping in the loft, seven sleeping people, not possible to open a window, seven individuals who breathe and smell.

He opens his eyes. Bárður is dead and everything grows cold.

Closes his eyes again.

Life can be very inconsiderate.

He is heavy with melancholy, his heart aches yet he has to pee so badly that everything else gives way to that need. So much so that he dares not cough, dares not even cry because the slightest exertion could press on his bursting bladder and cause something to leak out. This shows how much of an idiot I am, he thinks, and can lose himself for a moment in self-contempt, but he who needs to pee needs naturally to pee, and if he waits long enough the need becomes plainly overwhelming. He pulls himself slowly out of bed, he is naked, who could have undressed me, he thinks worriedly while he kneels down and searches around under the bed for the chamber pot, sighs when his hand collides with it. He pees on his knees so none of it misses the pot and it's good, it's so good to pee that he sighs contentedly and thus betrays his sorrow for the third time in a short while, he is a fool. He sits on the edge of the bed, looks straight ahead with little hope and breathes in the warm smell of urine. Silence around him, not even the sea is heard. His eyes have just started to get used to the lack of light, he sees the outline of two windows behind a heavy curtain, it's likely calm outside so they'll row. Pétur used the day yesterday to find two itinerant fishermen who now sit on the mid-thwart in place of Bárður and himself, while Andrea is doubtless worried about him, I need to write to her, yes, of course, but to tell her what? A trembling seizes his thin body, not strong but hardened by toil, cool in the room, he pulls the blanket over his shoulders and looks around. Much still hidden or hazy in the darkness but he has truly never slept alone in such a large space, except of course when he slept outside, under the bare sky. The bed has high ends, there he can distinguish a commode with six, no seven, drawers, and the outlines of pictures on the walls. There's a chair that looks nice to sit in. The boy glances around for his clothing, he is quite sad but still wants very much to try the chair. Could it be fake? And who removed his clothes? Helga, no doubt. It's not a particularly pleasant thought. So she's the first woman to see him naked. It could have been another woman, for example Guðrún. He tries to think about her, tries to miss her, but feels nothing, almost as if she means nothing to him. He stands up, goes to one of the windows, pulls the heavy curtain back and the cloudy April light streams over him, sweeps the darkness away and unveils the room. His clothes lie on a blue wooden chair next to the bed. He dresses, sniffs like a dog at the clothing, it has never smelled so good before, then stands for a long time over the heavy armchair, strokes it, over the wide arms, mutters something and then sits down carefully. The chair is incredibly soft and it is so absurdly good to sit in it that the boy smiles instinctively, but immediately bites his lips hard.

Bright outside and the night gone.

The April night is of course not very dark and it's also full of good sounds, one can hear running water, birdsong, flies, one can see earthworms in the dirt and life becomes more simple, April comes to us with a first-aid kit and tries to heal the wounds of winter.

The boy sits in the softest chair in the world and looks around, out the window and at the blue-white April clouds, tries to think about God but quickly gives up and regards the chamber pot instead, half full of cooling urine, white and so pure it's as if it's never been used. No, nor has he ever seen such a fine chamber pot before, just as well he couldn't see it properly when he peed, would surely not have dared to pee into such an elegant basin. Two paintings hang on the walls, rather large, he squints to distinguish the subjects, a city in one of them, foreign countries, he mutters. Just imagine, we live in a country where there is no city, no railroad, no palace, and besides we live so far from the world that many people don't know we exist. And is there anything to know? The other painting is less clear, he would need to stand up and move closer to get a good view, but that is naturally out of the question, it is much better to continue sitting there, looking around. I've probably slept for a good twenty-four hours, he thinks, feels it in his body, which is heavy, almost numb. Something makes a creaking sound near the boy, he is startled and for one deceitful moment he fears that Bárður is standing in the half-lit corner, looking at him. There are footsteps outside the door and someone laughs, a man but surely not the old captain, this is younger laughter, deep, almost cheerful, and besides the old man hardly ever laughs, just growls maybe. To his delight the boy feels his antipathy to Kolbeinn spread throughout his body. Old bugger, he mutters. The man laughs again and he hears a woman's voice. Incredible, folk do exist who laugh so early in the morning. The boy stands up, pulls the heavy curtains away from the other window, rather large windows latched together with hasps, he opens them and gulps in the cold, still morning air, it hasn't snowed since he walked or tottered into this house, he looks up and at the mountain towering above the Village. The morning light isn't completely clear, it's as if it is filled with impurities. Will it ever be completely bright beneath such a mountain? The boy backs away instinctively from the window and shuts it, it had quickly become chilly in the room, he wishes most to crawl into the bed again, cover his head, because what lies ahead, other than drawing breath, eating, going regularly to the privy, reading books, replying when spoken to? Why does a man live? He tries to say these words out loud, as if he were laying the question before God or maybe just before this fine chair, but since neither God nor the chair seem inclined to reply he starts thinking about Kolbeinn's books. They probably number around four hundred and he has never seen more than twenty books in the same place, except naturally at the Pharmacy, counted seventy-two when he was there with Bárður: four hundred books. He stares dreamily into space. Again the man laughs, but at more of a distance this time, just catches the distant sound, he rouses himself, stands up, goes quickly to the door, opens it, looks carefully out, a long hallway appears. He has surely slept for a long time behind the weighty curtains, but now he is awake and needs to find out why he is alive and whether there is in any sense room for him in this life.

He hesitates at the door. Looks over the large room, says good-bye to it, finally closes the door carefully behind him and walks slowly to the other end of the hallway. He counts five doors apart from the one he shut and four lamps on the walls, only two of them lit, thus it's half dark in the hallway, he peers at the pictures nearest to the glowing lamps. All foreign countries, he mutters after examining them, alien lakes, forests, palaces, cities. He goes very slowly down the stairs, the two voices carry up from below, he stops in the centre of the stairs, shuts his eyes, takes a deep breath and prepares himself. It's easy to deceive oneself in solitude, one can almost create a personality, become wise, reflective, have an answer to everything, but it's a different story in the company of others, you're put to the test, there you're not as reflective, not nearly as wise, you're sometimes a damned fool and say all sorts of stupid things. I'm sure I'll make a fool of myself, thinks the boy and continues down the stairs, counts sixteen steps. A closed door to his right when he comes down, a somewhat long hallway to the left leading to the main door, which is half open, and there stands a man, doubtless the one who laughed, rather tall, strong-looking, with broad shoulders, wearing a blue jacket with numerous gold buttons, a foreign ship captain, thinks the boy, one can also see it in how he carries himself, the combination of determination and carelessness, this man isn't dependent on saltfish and hasn't needed to live beneath the darkness of the mountains. The captain catches sight of the boy, who still holds onto the handrail because we often have to hold onto something in order not to get lost or tumble over the edge, it can be a handrail but preferably another hand. Their eyes meet, the foreigner's pucker as if he's on the look-out or perhaps just to see better. Helga steps into the hallway, had been standing in the doorway next to the captain, looks at the boy and says, good day, you slept. He lets go of the handrail but grabs it again and both agrees and bids her good day by nodding his head. It's possible to say much with a little movement of the head, words are likely overvalued, we should perhaps throw most of them out, just nod, whistle and hum. Helga looks at the captain and says something in a foreign language, speaks slowly but without hesitation, explaining who I am, thinks the boy, the skipper looks at him, no longer on his guard, and his face expresses sympathy, even pity. He sails the seas and knows death, thinks the boy, as if to justify to himself the warm currents the foreigner's glance releases within him. Then the captain nods at him, raises one of his arms, his hand is open and turned towards the boy, he glances suddenly upwards, it's as if he hesitates, as if he is waiting for something, but then he has gone out and the door has closed.

Well, says Helga.

Well is certainly the most important word there is in Icelandic, it can connect two strangers in an instant.

The boy walks over to her and she says, now you need to eat, and he says, yes.

VII

It's difficult to get to grips with Helga, Bárður had said as they walked away from the Village thirteen thousand years ago, with a perilous epic poem on his back, you're equally uncertain whether she simply tolerates you or whether she likes you, whether she's bored with life or not, dammit, sometimes I want to jump at her, shouting, just to throw her off balance and find out whether we can catch a glimpse of the real her, whoever that might be.

But Bárður's not about to jump at anyone now and say bah! Which is a good thing, really, because he is dead, frozen to death, and life recedes further from him with every passing minute, after thirty years he'll be at most a dull memory in the world, and then I'll also be completely forgotten, luckily. That's how the boy thinks, or rather, these thoughts flash within him as he follows Helga and tries to hold his anxiety and shyness at bay. Why should I be shy of her? Helga is just a person, her body is delicate and can't bear a landslide, can't bear time, time blinks and she's a decrepit old woman in a corner, munching on tasteless memories and names no-one else recalls.

135

The way from the hallway into the kitchen is barely ten steps, yet this all manages to flash through his head, there are clearly great expanses in the mind of a man, magnificent opportunities but most of them disused because existence stiffens quickly into the commonplace and opportunities diminish with every passing year, a large part of the mind is lost or turns to sandy wastes.

Helga is just under medium height, with quick, precise movements, she likely only knows the verb *to hesitate* by reputation. Her pale blonde hair is tied in a hard, firm knot at her neck, lending her face a sharp appearance, emphasizes her rather thin lips and her slightly upturned nose, she is wearing a loose light blue dress, the boy is uncertain of her physique, nor does he have any interest in it, she must be at least thirty years old.

They have come into the kitchen and all of the boy's restless thoughts and musings drop like shot birds, because there sits old Kolbeinn. Chewing a slice of bread with a thick layer of butter and pâté, his dead eyes slip through the boy like cold hands, and the events in the Café, his sheepishness, a word in Coddish, *Omaúnu*, stir slightly in his memory and begin immediately to mock him. He's awake, the kid, says Helga to the captain, who grunts something gruff in return like an old ram, he's seldom cheerful in the mornings, she explains to the boy, who has no idea whether he's expected to smile or not. Kolbeinn is such a perceptive man, she continues, that a long time ago he realized it's useless to be cheerful, generally speaking. The boy thinks of sitting down and then changes his mind, just stands there and wants desperately to make a face at the scowling captain but doesn't dare, instead watches Helga cut bread with deft movements, then the coffee starts to boil. The boy looks with great interest at the oven standing on four massive iron feet, with a hob and four plates for pots of different sizes. He has never seen such a large oven, scrutinizes the decorations on it and thus keeps himself occupied for a moment. Sit down, says Helga, without turning, and he does so immediately. Still, Kolbeinn is cheerful by nature, she says, and has even sung for me in the mornings. Again the munching captain grunts. Helga puts the bread and coffee on the table before the boy, who senses her warm bodily scent and ventures to smile, yet hesitantly, the heavily bearded captain's face opposite him reminds him of a dark cloudbank but there is a peculiar calmness over his work-fatigued hands that lie on the table like sleeping dogs, large compared to his body. The boy slurps the hot coffee, takes a bite of the bread and then hunger flares up so intensely that he needs to concentrate hard on not shoving all this soft bread into his mouth, forces himself to eat slowly, his surroundings demand more courtesy and elegant table manners than he is used to. Helga brings porridge in a blue bowl, he looks up, says instinctively, thank you, and so sincerely that she smiles a fleeting smile that reaches his eyes, giving him the courage to ask about the man who was leaving, is he a foreigner? Yes, she says, pours herself coffee in a blue cup, sits at the end of the table, captain of the other ship lying in the Lagoon, they're sailing later, he's English, she adds and sips her coffee. Do you know English, he asks carefully and respectfully, because whoever knows another language must see farther and know more than other people. Some, I lived in America for six years, but he's not here to visit me or admire my English. Why does he come then, asks the boy, so innocent, but just for one moment, sees almost immediately through the innocence, or the idiocy, and turns bright red. Helga purses her lips, either from displeasure or to keep herself from smiling, Kolbeinn's face is blank. The boy shovels the porridge into his mouth, thereby preventing himself from putting his foot in it.

It's best to get going.

Already returned the book, mission accomplished, thank you very much, next on the schedule is to decide whether he should live or die. Refreshing when one's choices are limited to two and are so decisive. Of course it's considerably simpler to die, just one decision and then everything's finished, get a piece of rope, tie it around a stone, hop off a cliff and never come back up, no-one would need to stumble upon his stranded corpse.

It's entirely more complicated to live.

It won't do to get a piece of rope, even if it were a very good piece of rope, one needs more than that to live, life is a long and complicated process, to live is to question. Where, for example, should he stay the next night, the next nights, the next ten thousand nights? And he needs to find work, he's not going to sea, fuck that, no, and he's not going to work at Leó's Shop in the summer, not without Bárður, out of the question. But what then, he needs to eat, it costs money. He could conceivably make a deal with

Magnús' Shop or Tryggvi's Shop for moderate credit, the ships will sail soon and then there'll be more than enough to do and any workers very welcome. Yes, yes, of course it's not a problem to take necessary provisions out on credit for a few days, no problem to survive, but entirely more complicated to figure out whether he has, in general, any business in this world.

That's how the boy thinks, has finished his porridge, holds his empty spoon and stares at nothing, no self-pity in his face but perhaps a touch of helplessness, because how is he supposed to get some rope? One doesn't find it in the street, life will always put obstacles in our way, nothing is ever easy. Bárður never had any problems with anything, yet he died and will never again laugh that infectious laugh of his.

The boy is startled, Helga is saying something. What? he asks but she shakes her head and mutters, so I'm left with a deaf man and a blind man. The boy looks swiftly at Kolbeinn but there is no Kolbeinn there, he's simply gone. I just, says the boy, falls silent as he searches for more words but doesn't find them, has lost all of them.

You lose your hearing, get it back and then lose your voice, you're truly exciting to be around, says Helga, and he naturally has no idea whether she's saying this cheerfully or sarcastically, once again he's uncertain and fearful of this woman and thus agrees silently, with a movement of his head, to go out with her and down to Tryggvi's Shop. We need milk, beer, porridge, bread, I need a pack-animal, deaf or mute, it doesn't matter, but hopefully your strength doesn't disappear as suddenly from your arms.

VIII

The sky is no longer cold as frost over the world, the snow has started to soften in the street, it is April. And here he walks.

Helga says nothing, luckily, as if she's left all her words behind at the house, Geirþrúður wants to speak to you later, was the last thing she said, while they were putting on their coats. Later? he asked, as if this word, *later*, were completely incomprehensible, she doesn't like getting up early, Helga had said, and ignored the boy's inquisitive look, why does she want to talk to me, he thinks out in the street, maybe to blame me for not having saved Bárður from the frost? Helga walks so quickly that he has to use all his strength to keep up and his line of thinking is constantly tearing apart. This street is called Moon Street, he thinks. We'll walk to the end of it and then Sea Street starts and goes all the way to the Point, but there's the churchyard, should I maybe whistle to the dead and invite them out for a walk? They've cleared a decent path along the road and an even better one in Sea Street, besides the snow there is packed and it's no trouble at all to walk on it. It's fairly bright in the sky despite the heavy clouds, the hour is likely near 7.00, the sea blue and slightly rough out in the fjord, likely near freezing. The boy has warmed up during their walk, it seems not to matter how long his strides are, he is always at least half a step behind Helga. Smoke ascends from the chimneys of the houses that stand next to Magnús' drying lot, three men smoke pipes outside the shop, likely foreign fishermen, the masts on the two ships rise into the air at Lower Pier down at the Point, the ships themselves hidden behind the buildings. One of the ships is called *St Lovisa*, it comes from England, Captain J. Andersen and his body still warm after nights and days with Geirþrúður. The smoke from the pipes of the three men ascends into the sky, blue but dissipates quickly, turns to nothing. The boy looks at the masts that rise above the houses in the morning air, I should go to America, flashes in his mind, of course, that's the answer, or Canada, which is a very large country. Then I would come a very long way from the sea, from the fish, I would learn English and could read important books. He wants to think more about this but his thoughts dissipate in the air like smoke. The road branches before them, Sea Street continues along the sea but Main Street curves past the corner of Magnús' Shop and shoves its way in between a dense row of houses. The streets here have been shovelled well, the road is almost empty, with snow piles on both sides. There are eight, no nine, houses of varying stateliness on both sides of Main Street and two little spruces peek up from the snow in front of one of the better houses, so absurdly green that the boy stops abruptly. He longs to clamber over the snow piles to touch this green colour and

141

smell its fragrance. He looks up and sees a woman in the window above the trees, she is young, appears to be polishing something, a candlestick, it seems to him, and she looks at him, then smiles so beautifully that he suddenly feels happiness, yet Bárður froze to death by his side forty-eight hours ago. Confused, he tears himself away from the window with two living eyes and a smile and runs off after Helga, who is disappearing around the corner, he runs and runs fast, as fast as he can, as if he were trying to catch up with himself, looks a fool, naturally, which is excellent because that is precisely what he is.

Main Street goes to the centre of the Village, Central Square, which is what we call it when we dream of life without saltfish, dream of a square with trees, benches and statues, but statues of whom, that is the question, because who has been so faithful to life that he deserves a statue?

Central Square is covered with April snow and will doubtless be like that for the next several days, there is snowfall in these clouds and the sun will hardly show itself today. Few people out and about, in fact just these two, the boy winded at Helga's side, he didn't manage to escape from himself. Window curtains move in the house above them, a face looks out. Sometimes very little happens here and folk run to the window if they sense any movement, merely waking and thinking of the day ahead makes you sleepy. Helga heads for Tryggvi's Shop, a big house neatly labelled with a large sign, long windows full to the brim with goods in the summer and fall, but sparse now. A man comes out with a little bag of sticks under his arm, glances at Helga without, however, saying hello, she pretends not to see him and opens the door, they step into the shop and the bell rings.

IX

The boy blinks to accustom his eyes to the difference in the light.
It seems half dark in here after the brightness of the snow outside.
A handful of people in the shop, shop staff and customers, and
everyone stops talking as Helga and the boy come in, innumerable
eyes that look first at her, then at him, curious, investigative eyes,
some even hostile and it's not nice at all to be gawped at in such
a way. Good floor, will you swallow me up, thinks the boy, but
is however rather sceptical because floors have never swallowed
anyone up, floors don't actually know anything but how to be
flat and walked upon. It would thus be better for him to have a look
around, regard the selection of goods in the largest shop in the
Village, the largest that has ever been seen in this part of the country, one needs to go south to Reykjavík to visit a more remarkable
shop, or even all the way to Copenhagen, across the wide sea that
is dangerously deep, full of sunken ships, drowned folk, dashed
hopes. He has of course come here before, thrice in two years. But
everything looked different then, because certain people were
alive at that time. The April light comes in through the windows,

neither hard nor particularly strong. Several paraffin lamps are lit but the shop is large, and four tall and broad cabinets break up the space, create shadows, make it more difficult for the light. The counter is long, many metres in length, and behind it are shelves displaying various goods, some empty because we're waiting for more spring ships, the two ships at Lower Pier only brought coal, salt and a captain for Geirþrúður. The boy has counted nine people there when the tenth, a tall, well-built man, appears at the end of one of the cabinets, had been examining something but wishes to check who the newcomers are and stares for a long time at the boy, this is Brynjólfur, captain of the ship attached to Snorri's Shop, his beard dark and grizzled, the boy looks away from the dark, almost black eyes and looks in through the open door of the liquor room. The boy went in there with Bárður fifty thousand years ago, when mammoths roamed the earth. At that time the shelves were nearly empty. The cognac was finished, the whiskey was finished, the sherry was finished, five bottles left of port, ten of *brennivín*, two of Svensk-Branco, nine bottles of red wine, this was how the possibilities of life had diminished. But there were still dense rows of several types of beer and more than enough in the warehouse, the shop assistant had said, had looked at Bárður and the boy as if from a distance, leaned back to emphasize the difference between him and them and the smile beneath the most neatly trimmed moustache the boy had ever seen, not at all free of arrogance. Bárður asked for *brennivín*, huh, what? not red wine? asked the assistant, as if in surprise. Bárður had it put on his account, easy enough, his account was in good order, the moustache also said, yes, this is fine, after looking Bárður up, and the distance between them diminished slightly, from seven hundred kilometres down to two hundred. The boy was filled with pride, stood up straight while Bárður simply extended his strong arm, I'll take it like this, and they walked out, the neck of the bottle in Bárður's grasp, drank it down to the shoulder on the way out to the fishing station but Bárður never drank any more wine in this life. Now that damned Einar is gaping his mouth over the bottle, thinks the boy, eyeing it greedily like a starved seagull.

The thought of Einar, his greed and indifference to Bárður's death, makes the boy so angry that his shyness is momentarily alleviated and he walks over to the counter where Helga asks for goods, speaks quietly but determinedly and without any sign of hesitation, or submission for that matter, in her manner.

Oh, how everything in this world is divided unequally.

Some people can stand like that at a shop counter and say without hesitation, I want this and that, and the assistants go obediently wherever they point, while the rest of us have to ask, request whether it would be all right to add this, and that, and say that it would be so lovely to have a handful of raisins, God help me, not to mention Danish boiled sweets! Then we smile feebly into the face of the person behind the counter, on pins and needles over whether she will pull out the big black book with the red spine where all our debits are recorded, our debts to society and men written in immovable numbers that are impossible to dispute, you just give in. Most of us are eternally in debt to the big shops, and of course also to life itself, but that debt is paid with death. The case is not so simple as far as Tryggvi's Shop is concerned, there the sins of the fathers pass down to their descendants, because although death is a powerful bastard its power doesn't extend to account ledgers; if the man dies the wife pays, the children, parents. This has nothing to do with cruelty but rather with business, it's just reality, that's how reality is. Tryggvi's Shop and Leó's Shop are so big that the Village stands and falls with them, their disciplined and thoroughgoing management keeps everything running, sustains us, heedlessness in management, irresolution, and we're finished, the Village and its residents would fall into destitution. Friðrik has said this many times and we would rather not dispute him, except under our breath, as when we say our prayers. He has a majority of the town council under his wing, or perhaps in his shadow, and few decisions are made without getting his opinion on them one way or another. But Helga doesn't need to curtsey and smile nervously. She just sticks her hand in her pocket and pays cash. Those who are in the shop, some to buy things, others just to loiter, pass the time, have waited for this moment ever since Helga walked in. Money, pay cash, the moment has a kind of dreamy sweetness. Add two cases of beer, says Helga to the female shop assistant, who turns to her co-worker, the moustache himself, who bows humbly and says, of course, we just need to get it from the warehouse, then we'll deliver it up to the Café. He looks first at the assistant, who is called Ragnheiður and is Friðrik's daughter, neither more nor less, and then at Helga and smiles courteously. Then go get the cases, says Helga, almost coldly, doesn't even look once at the moustache, the smile vanishes from his face, he says, of course we'll do that and looks quickly at two other assistants standing near him and following the proceedings, they hop to it and head out to the warehouse.

The bell rings again above the door and a tall, slim woman walks in. She has brown eyes like the man who froze to death because of lines of poetry. Hello, Þorunn, Helga says to the woman and smiles, Þorunn smiles back, goes over to Helga and they hug. The boy is flabbergasted to see Helga so cheerful, but once again becomes insecure and somehow lost, because the two women, Helga and this Þorunn, walk over to one of the windows to speak together, leaving him standing alone at the counter. Ragnheiður and the moustache, who is called Gunnar, both look at him, then she turns and reaches for a glass of water. They both watch as she raises the glass to her lips and empties it.

She drinks slowly. Her small larynx moves like a sleepy little animal in her white neck.

A dull sound of bells carries to them from the liquor room. Gunnar curses quietly, opens his mouth and appears to be on the verge of saying something to Ragnheiður but either decides not to say it or doesn't dare. She doesn't take her eyes off the boy, as if she is curious, as if she can't pull her eyes off him. Gunnar looks at him suddenly, with a heavy and hostile expression, then goes into the liquor room, heeding the bell.

It was the captain, Brynjólfur, who had taken the opportunity when everyone's attention was directed at Þorunn and Helga, gone into the liquor room, rung the bell extremely carefully and now shuffles his feet restlessly when he sees Gunnar's heavy expression. The floor creaks beneath the captain's huge feet. It would take a god to bring down Brynjólfur, we sometimes say, because he's withstood all the raging weather of the sea, when the sky appears about to be ripped apart, the waves rise dozens of metres above the ship, the air is filled with a maddening whine and everything unfixed vanishes overboard, the men are tossed to and fro down in the forecastle, which is filling with seawater, and everything is soaked, and there stands Brynjólfur firm as a rock on those giant feet, hands on the helm, smiling, even laughing in the face of the terror, shouting with delight, some have said, shouting with wild happiness. But in such Doomsday weather one can still hear nothing but the maddening whine of the storm, then the sound when the waves break, crash over the ship, which shakes from end to end, and the most experienced fishermen break with the waves, weep from fear and defencelessness down in the hold, but Brynjólfur stands at the helm with that ominous grin. Those who have looked up from the hold and seen him appear briefly in the midst of the spray maintain that his face radiates happiness, a happy, heathen expression, an old fisherman once said. But it's of course one thing to stand unaffected before the threats of the elements and another to long for beer, to long so much for beer that it almost hurts, and another to be in considerable debt to the shop and because of that entirely subject to Gunnar's whims. Indecipherable, this Gunnar. Brynjólfur decides to be modest: it wouldn't be bad getting four or five beers off you, dear Gunnar, he says, puts on a tender, even pious expression to counteract the voice that by its nature has little space for modesty. What do you want with beer? asks Gunnar brusquely, looking derisively at the captain. Brynjólfur laughs hesitantly, as if he were holding a delicate bomb, that's a good question, he says, and tries to be companionable, what does a man do with beer!

What does a man do with beer; if only the world revolved around drinking or not drinking beer, if only it were so simple.

Ragnheiður gives the boy a shamefully undisguised look, as if she were feeling him with her eyes, and he has no idea what to do with himself.

What, for example, should he do with these hands, so long and ugly and constantly getting in his way?

What is he supposed to do with these idiotic eyes?

Or these grotesque feet?

And who might you be? asks Ragnheiður after he has suffered for several seconds, each second around a hundred years. There may be curiosity in her voice, but also a great deal of haughtiness. The boy needs to gather his courage to look into Ragnheiður's face, and that he does, gathers courage and looks into her face. Two auburn curls have fallen down around her temples. Her eyes are as grey as the rock faces in some places in the mountains, difficult to look into them but it's also very difficult to ignore them. She's beautiful, thinks the boy in surprise.

And he is entirely correct.

Ragnheiður has worked in the shop for three years, we first said, yes, Friðrik's girl, the apple of his eye, the emperor's daughter, but that soon stopped when we realized that in a certain sense she wasn't the daughter of anyone but herself and made decisions without consulting her father. Some people feared her even more than Friðrik. She has denied people credit in the dead of winter when the cold has penetrated the houses and everything freezes that can freeze, liquids and hope, and all the food nearly gone, but Ragnheiður simply points at the high level of debt and the frivolous debits, sweets, tobacco and again tobacco, *brennivín*, figs, she chills the person in question to the bone with her eyes. Her voice can be sharp and can cleave full-grown men, hardened by the sea, from their shoulders right down. Yet she is only twenty-one years old and life sometimes quivers within her.

The boy certainly gets a hard and cold feeling from her, but that simply charms him in a strange, unexplainable way. Queen of the Polar Sea, he thinks, and loses himself entirely in her eyes, forgets everything but her stone-grey eyes in her petite face, framed by her auburn hair. Ragnheiður leans forward a bit and says quietly, maybe you're mute? Did Geirþrúður want to get herself a mute since she already had a blind man? The boy feels the blush spreading over his cheeks, say something, you fool, he orders himself, there's no need to come across as a complete idiot even though you are one. He looks away, having gone far towards turning completely beet-red, but then sets his eyes on *The Will of the People*, our newspaper, which lies folded on the counter-top. *Still Iced Over on the Baltic Sea*, is the front-page headline, *Laura remains trapped in the ice with goods and packages for Iceland*. Frozen solid with all the letters from students in Copenhagen, some so hot with homesickness and admissions of love that it would certainly be enough to let them dangle off the prow to melt the ice and clear the water. Something stirs in the boy's heart. He looks again into the stone-grey eyes and says, so softly that Ragnheiður has to lean even farther forward to hear, I just don't know who I am. I don't know why I am. And I am not entirely sure that I'll be given time to find out.

Why in the hell did I say that? he thinks in confusion and tries not to look too much at the white breasts partly revealed when she leans forward. Ragnheiður straightens up, there is a trace of uncertainty in her face but then the tip of her tongue appears unexpectedly between her lips, red and glistening with moisture.

A tip of a tongue that appears in this way seems to carry with it a message from within, from within the darkness of the body.

Dammit, thinks the boy.

The stone-grey eyes run slowly, very slowly, down his body. Eyes are invisible hands that stroke, feel, touch, find. Then she smiles. It is a deliberate, haughty smile, yet seems to quiver a tiny bit, almost invisibly, when she says, you should get some proper clothing. And you should straighten up a bit, then I'll talk to you better. But don't you dare try to say hello to me in the street!

Then there is nothing but the counter between them.

The boy had, without realizing it, moved closer, wanting to discover how she smelled, her scent, we're more courageous when we think nothing, the hesitation, the nervousness, come with thinking. He's like an animal and comes so close to her that he can hear her breathe. The tip of her tongue appears again, momentarily, a message to him from the darkness, then she takes a step back, her eyes turn cold and haughty and giant icebergs rise between them.

X

Þorunn's a good person, and she's invaluable company for Geirþrúður and me, Helga says as they walk from the shop, she with one bag, he with loads, grateful for the weight, he who bears a burden can forget himself in the exertion, rest his mind, and uncertainty doesn't tear him to shreds in the meantime. Uncertainty about life, about what is to come, about himself and now also Ragnheiður, this girl with the stone-grey eyes, the tip of her tongue, her breasts, incomprehensibly enchanting in her haughtiness and coldness, cold as pack ice, why did I have to fall for an iceberg? A good person and valuable company, says Helga about Þorunn and appears about to add something, perhaps tell the boy something about this Þorunn, and the boy is astonished at how open, almost talkative, Helga has become, but then they hear heavy footsteps approaching, it's good to carry something heavy, says a dusky, sonorous voice, and Brynjólfur strides past the boy, slaps him heavily on the shoulder. The captain has three bottles of beer in his pockets, and therefore life is pretty good. Four or five bottles would naturally have been even better, but

Gunnar was so damned grumpy and curt that it would have been a bad idea to ask for more. Brynjólfur greets Helga cheerfully and is going to stride past her but she stops the giant by putting out her hand, he seems to grow agitated, reaches instinctively into his pocket for a beer, opens the bottle and takes a gulp. Weren't you supposed to be on board your ship a long time ago, preparing it to sail, Helga says more than asks, the other captains are well into their preparations, but your ship is still lying there on the beach while you loaf in the shops and drink beer, that's not very considerate to Snorri. Brynjólfur raises one of his arms, heavy with striking power, enormous strength, but he can also raise it gently, and then his open palm is like an apologetic smile. Helga snorts and Brynjólfur says, somewhat enthusiastically, I'm starting today, my dear, I'm starting today! I'd like for you to stick to your word, she says simply and walks away with the boy behind her. Brynjólfur winks at him, takes another swig of beer, goes first in the opposite direction from them but then turns down another street, the boy and Helga continue in the direction of Geirþrúður's house, he thankful for getting to carry such weight, trying not to think more about Ragnheiður, about the breasts that stretched towards him when she leaned forward, about the tip of her tongue glistening with moisture, about the stone-grey eyes, cold and repellant but at the same time so enchanting. She is a huge iceberg, he thinks, a huge iceberg with polar bears that tear me into pieces and eat me. But when he finally manages to push her out of his thoughts, the questions about life come at him, about whether he should live, and then why, and whether he deserves to.

Oh, uncertainty is a bird shrieking above his head.

Now we shall simply leave him alone, just for a moment, and maybe for a moment more. Just allow him to be at one with his burden, leave him in peace and instead follow this captain, Brynjólfur, as he saunters in the direction of Snorri's Shop, taking his sweet time.

A person carrying three beers doesn't have much need to hurry in this world.

XI

If you take the shortest path to Snorri's Shop from Central Square and don't dawdle, it should take you around five minutes. But that is of course an unnecessarily short amount of time now, because it's so good to drink beer, absolutely unbelievably good, what was a short time ago heavy and unconquerable becomes a breeze. Now I'll start preparing the ship, says Brynjólfur to himself, says it out loud, informs the world of this decision of his, punches himself in the chest, a mighty blow, does it both to beat his chest and to encourage himself. First he'll go to Snorri, arrange things with him, they'll make plans, enjoy the moment together, perhaps toast each other over a strong drink, then he'll walk with a lantern down to the ship, wake it from its heavy winter sleep, have his moments with it and wake the crew in the morning. Yes! Brynjólfur punches himself in the chest again, happily, victoriously, the one captain who hasn't started to prepare his ship for the fishing season, the others far ahead and soon to sail, but the ship of Brynjólfur and the merchant Snorri still sleeps at the edge of the beach, lies there clumsily, like a flightless bird. Brynjólfur hasn't even looked once in its direction, despite Snorri having twice urged him, in his hesitant, apologetic way, completely useless at coaxing people, which is no good because his shop stands on shaky feet, its outstanding debts outnumbering its assets. Those who owe are mostly common labourers living in the old neighbourhood, fishermen, renters, a farmer or two. Some have difficulties paying, while others perhaps don't put much effort into work and consciously or unconsciously take advantage of Snorri's irresolution and kindness, which he frequently tries to suppress but with little success, kindness in one person can evoke rottenness in others. Snorri has his best moments at an old, tired organ, and he also feels fine when he sings in church on New Year's Eve, Easter Sunday, at midsummer, when he sings in praise of light, as Reverend Þorvaldur calls it, and those who owe money to Snorri, some with debts of many years, feel a bit ashamed, yet that's an ache that everyday life erases. It is the ship's catch on which Snorri relies, Brynjólfur knows that very well, and perhaps that is why he punches himself on the chest for the third time as he turns down School Street, knows he already should have come a long way in preparing his ship, it is called *The Hope*, a beautiful and bright name, a fifteen-year-old ship Snorri bought new from Norway. It was first named *Jón Sigurðsson* after the staid hero of Icelandic independence, but then Snorri had it hauled up to the edge of the beach and got Bjarni the painter to paint *The Hope* in red on the bow. A few days earlier Snorri's wife had gone aboard the *Thyra* south to Reykjavík, so advanced in her illness that she needed to be carried on board. Of course Snorri went with her, but had to return here to the west on the next boat to keep the company operating smoothly.

And months passed.

Jens, then newly appointed as overland postman, delivered letters from her, but they grew shorter and shorter as the summer passed, the handwriting weaker and less legible. Snorri peered at the crooked and distorted words, the shaky handwriting witnessing his wife's dwindling vitality. *Oh, it's become a bit difficult now,* she wrote in a letter at the start of August, the first words of complaint to come from her, *I sometimes awake with cold hands inside me. They are colder than ice, and move closer to my heart every day. Dear Snorri, if worse comes to worst, if God calls me to him, then you must be strong. You must not break. Think of our boys. I trust that you will get them into school, as we have always planned … but now I cannot write more … my beloved husband.* Or he thought he saw those words there at the end, *my beloved husband,* although to be sure it was incredibly unlike her to express herself so openly, display her affection with such naked words. Snorri locked himself in his office so he could weep without running the risk of anyone discovering him. It was two weeks until the coastal boat would stop here on its way south and Snorri couldn't wait that long, life wasn't so long, good men loaned him two horses and he galloped off, rode straight into the fjord and up the Tungudalur Valley, the horses spirited, strong, but he like a cry of desperation on the back of one of them.

If God calls me to him.

Snorri returned a month later. It was September. He got caught in winter weather on the heaths but came down into the valley in happy sunshine and birdsong, perfect calm and 15 degrees Celsius, returned the horses, thanked the creatures by putting his arms around their necks, and the horses rubbed their large heads against the merchant, then he went home to see to raising the boys and running the shop. For a long time no-one dared speak to him about anything but common matters and what the language could deal with easily, about fish, the shop, the weather. It was mainly those who were interested in music and who could connect with Snorri by means of those ties who could come anywhere near him, yet that wasn't much. Jens clearly knew something but felt it useless to spread it around and folk saw quickly that it could be dangerous to press him on the matter, his face would grow dark and his large fists would clench and folk would hurry to change the topic. We're thus unsure of certain small details; all we know is that God certainly called her to himself. Some clearly have ears for his voice, while we, who ramble here, dead yet still alive, listen and listen but never hear anything. But God spoke to her. And then laid his hand over her abdomen, where the pain was worst and the hands coldest, and when Snorri came to Reykjavík, exhausted and sleep-deprived on worn-out horses, his wife Aldís received him in full health, the pain gone and a peculiar light shining from her. Snorri was actually half wary of her, something unconquerable had risen between them and nothing was like it had been before.

Snorri tried everything he could to bring her home, but what is a man's word when God has spoken? Three weeks later he rode home, but Aldís sailed to Copenhagen and started to do the work proscribed to her by God.

Jens delivers two letters a year from Aldís. They don't go through the hands of Dr Sigurður because Jens gives them to Snorri in person, and these dispassionately written letters are full of godly light that illuminates the face of the merchant and the beard that has grizzled greatly. But all light casts shadows, that's just how it is, and it's in the shadow of the light of God that Snorri lives, because in place of being happy and celebrating, he misses Aldís and is bitter towards God for having taken her from him. He expects that his ingratitude is great and sinful, I will burn in Hell for this, he sometimes thinks with remorse. Snorri plays the organ almost every day, Bach, Chopin, Mozart, but also some meandering melodies sprung from regret and guilt. Music is unlike everything else. It is the rain that falls in the desert, the sunshine that illuminates hearts, and it is the night that comforts. Music ties people together, so Snorri is not always alone when he pumps the organ, strokes the bow over the strings of an old fiddle, its highest note so thin and sharp that it can sunder hearts. Benedikt is sometimes with him, you remember, the skipper who blows the signal to depart, the Custodian waits at the seashore with three hundred fishermen all around. And there are more who come to Snorri for the music, women and men, but a person can sit surrounded by many and still be alone; it is first and foremost for his boys that

Snorri lives. They are the hope that keeps him afloat, both in the Learned School, one about to finish and determined to become a priest, the other wishes to go further, to Copenhagen, to study veterinary science, they live with their father during the summers and then he rediscovers happiness, and it's because of them that he toils away at the shop, fights an exhausting fight to keep it going, it's expensive to educate the boys, girls are cheaper to manage and have few opportunities for education, have little opportunity in general and lose their freedom simply by marrying.

Brynjólfur winces slightly. Not, however, because of the girls, their limited opportunities, but because of the responsibility that rests upon him, and his remorse, two birds sitting on his shoulders and shoving their claws deep into his flesh. But now everything's getting better, absolutely! After three or four hours he'll have come with his lantern down to *The Hope*, will have started to talk to the ship, started to make preparations. Tomorrow he'll wake the impatient crew and after that there'll be no slacking! Brynjólfur is glad, has started on his second beer and feels the third beer bottle in his right pocket, soon I'll drink it, he thinks with a smile, and walks past the school that the brothers Jón the joiner and Nikulás the carpenter, called Núlli, built in their time, a tall, rather narrow building, with three large windows on the front of the upper storey, so large it's as if the building eternally opens its eyes wide with wonder. The school was meant to be only one storey but we're no good at sticking to agreements, besides Núlli and Jón found it immensely enjoyable to build the school, they both dreamed of going to school in their youth and often told each other, now we're building for the children, now we're building for the future, their world should be better than ours, and because of this they added another storey. It is slightly narrower and it's a bit as if the building has not only opened its eyes wide but has also taken a deep breath. The town council would not agree to their ideas unconditionally and used lack of money as an excuse, but the brothers still had all the money they received for building the Tower House of Elías the Norwegian, a huge building located on Central Square, it was the first time they'd been paid cash and they kept the money at home, and neither had the heart to spend it or found a decent enough reason to do so. They then started constructing the school, and there they finally found a worthy project. Besides, we also had a lucky break: a ship carrying choice Norwegian timber was stranded not far from here, on its way to Akureyri. It had sought shelter from a storm, took its chance on the fjords, those tremendous jaws that gape open towards the Polar Sea, and never made it out again. Two crewmen drowned, their bodies were never found and thus they were added to the large group of fishermen who ramble about the seafloor, jabbering to each other about the jogtrot of time, waiting for the final call that someone had promised them in days of old, waiting for God to pull them up, fish them up with his net of stars, dry them off with his warm breath, permit them to walk with dry feet in Heaven, where one never eats fish, say the drowned, always just as optimistic, busy themselves with looking up at the boats, expressing amazement at the new fishing gear, cursing the rubbish that people leave behind in the sea, but sometimes weeping with regret for life, weeping as drowned folk weep, and that is why the sea is salty.

It was of course very bad that these men drowned, but the timber from the ship was a windfall that could likely be put to use for the upper storey of the elementary school.

Núlli died at the precise moment when he drove the final nail in, boomp! was heard as he struck the nail, boomp! was heard in his heart and then nothing more was ever heard from Núlli. He sank slowly forward, his forehead touched the side of the building next to the nail that stood halfway out and still does, in memory of a good carpenter, a noble fellow, so high up that we can't hang anything on it except raindrops and spiders' webs. It's not possible to say much about Núlli's life, it passed without any grand events, there weren't many stories about him and it wouldn't be entirely easy to write his obituary, yet we felt the emptiness long after he was gone. His brother Jón was naturally brokenhearted, they were unmarried, got on extremely well and had lived together, just the two of them, since their parents died. We sometimes found Jón crying out in the open or with his hammer in his hand over some project. This was heartrending and we were completely at a loss. We just watched how he pined away, nearly turned into a wretch from sorrow and regret and loneliness. It isn't an overstatement to say that he was well on the way to indigence when Gunnhildur, who had had a child by Reverend Þorvaldur, you recall their night together when he didn't take his cassock off, visited Jón in the rubbish bin that the brothers' apartment had become.

Well, dear Jón, she said, we two certainly are orphans in this world, I toil away over a little child whom the cassock-wretch refuses to have anything to do with, have no-one to support me, and no-one at all to talk to in the evenings, let alone anything else. And here you are alone, with your good heart. You can be such a tremendously hard worker but it's awful to see you now. I think you're wasting away from loneliness and regret. There's no shame in it, but it's also perfectly unnecessary. Look here, we could certainly continue to toil away on our own, I'll survive, not elegantly but I'll manage, and won't make my child feel ashamed, still it won't be easy and it won't be pretty. On the other hand, you, dear Jón, you can't manage on your own for long, you're just that way. You're a hard worker and a gem of a man but far too sensitive. God gave you a good and beautiful heart but completely forgot to harden it. You're losing everything, soon you'll lose the house, soon you'll lose your independence, finally you'll lose life itself. Why should we let that happen, what, I wonder, would be the purpose of that? What do you say, dear Jón, about my moving in here ... Gunnhildur looked around, Jón sat on a tattered chair and couldn't take his eyes off her face, her enormous number of freckles ... into this hole of yours, and together we make it into a good home? As far as love is concerned, naturally there's nothing to say, since we barely know one another, but I'm absolutely certain that in the future we'll grow fond of each other, and that, you see, is no small thing. I feel so strongly that I could easily grow very fond of you, you're a marvellous man, and to see the blueness in your eyes, I could completely forget myself looking at it! On the other hand I'm not nearly as good as you, I'm actually a damned trove of faults, yet not entirely bad, and I'm a terrifically hard worker and brutally honest. What do you say to that, dear Jón? I could be the hardening around your heart. My boy is unchristened, Reverent Tatterfrock isn't after me about it, imagine that, but suddenly I got the idea that Nikulás would be a stand-out name for the boy, and then Jónsson, if you're interested. By the way, don't you have any coffee for us, I'll brew it, you know how good it can be to think with a good cup of coffee in one's hands, I'm not used to speaking so much, by the way, I expect I'm a little bit nervous, yes, I see the coffee, there it is.

Shortly afterwards the house smelled of coffee. Jón the joiner got to kiss her on the mouth, she started to tidy immediately and then went to fetch the child from her girlfriend. Can't you sleep? asked Gunnhildur that night, had awakened to the child's crying, comforted it, rocked it back to sleep and then noticed that Jón was wide awake, lay there with wide-open eyes, scarcely daring to blink, can't you sleep? No, actually not, he said apologetically. Is it because of the child, do you want us to sleep in the parlour, I'll move us immediately! She pulled the cover off and was halfway out of bed when Jón placed his work-worn carpenter's hand carefully on her shoulder, no, he said shyly, don't go.

Brynjólfur shivers. He'd lost track of himself, leaned against a streetlight, looked at the school and let his mind wander, the air is chilly and it's cold to stand there motionless for a long time. The street lamp is extinguished as well. Bárður the night-watchman looks after our street lamps at night and extinguishes them when there's no longer any need for their light. There are not all that many street lamps in the Village, with long distances between them; they're actually like life: several gleaming moments set apart by dark days. Brynjólfur shivers, clears his throat, spits and then continues on his way. A child coughs in a nearby house, a long, hard cough, be good now, God, and watch over this life, Brynjólfur prays, then greets and smiles at two housekeepers walking towards him with water buckets on their way to the well, trusting that Bárður the nightwatchman has done his duty and broken the ice off the well cover during the night. Brynjólfur becomes so incomprehensibly happy at seeing the two women that he stops, flings his arms wide, transforms them into an embrace large enough to have room for both of them, if I weren't married, he says, I would kiss you both and then marry you! The two women smile at his words and at the neck of the bottle poking out of the captain's pocket. Are you man enough to be of use to two women? one of them says, it's Bryndís, she's lost two husbands to the sea and is raising three children, if you only knew, Brynjólfur says, and he laughs and grabs his crotch, yes, Bryndís says, but it's not just size that counts, the other giggles and then they've gone past him.

Brynjólfur turns to watch them walk away. Bryndís is almost a head taller, a combination of nobility, softness and tension in the way she walks, I love her, thinks Brynjólfur in surprise, and places both hands firmly over his left breast, as if to prevent his heart from tearing itself out of his chest cavity and pursuing Bryndís, the heart that at one time beat only for Ólafía, his wife, they've lived together for so many years that Brynjólfur doesn't want to think about it now and instead watches as Bryndís kneels down and removes the cover from the well. It's so sweet to look at this woman, perhaps the best thing there is in this life. But then she is finished filling the buckets, she smiles at Brynjólfur and is gone, the moment past.

Brynjólfur takes the stopper out of the last bottle, turns down School Street into Old Lane, thereby entering the old neighbourhood. Many of the oldest houses in the Village are located in this area, variously sized timber houses from the latter part of the eighteenth century. Most of the residents of the neighbourhood are simple fishermen or labourers, some with irritable hens in their backyards, and in some places their houses are so densely packed together that they almost touch each other. Those who have sailed to other countries, seen other worlds and woken up beneath foreign skies, surrounded by other languages, say that at its best the old neighbourhood resembles foreign cities with their innumerable confined, winding lanes. Folk from better classes choose, on the other hand, to avoid the neighbourhood, and it caused a great deal of amazement, if not scandal, when the and father, whom Brynjólfur knew well, they were childhood friends, and now he is dead. The memory of him stops Brynjólfur in his tracks, childhood friends are irreplaceable, that's why Brynjólfur feels compelled to finish his beer. There is often a kind of clear sky above childhood friends, light and innocence. Brynjólfur sighs over his memories and over his beer being finished. He has leaned against the fence outside the little timber house with its small addition that could be anything at all, really, a storehouse, toolshed, workroom, he knows the people who live there, a fisherman on one of the ships and his wife, they have five children, argue endlessly and curse each other, no-one understands what keeps them together but we will likely never understand this glue that can connect two different people their entire lives, so powerful that even hatred can't tear them apart. Brynjólfur regards his beer bottle, Gammel Carlsberg, it's so heart-breakingly empty and it has been so heartbreakingly long since he was a child. Brynjólfur looks down at his feet and mutters, there now, go on you two, and they obey, reluctantly, he walks slowly and thinks about his friend and thinks about his daughter, Bryndís, who lost them all in an instant: husband, father and brother. Her father was the skipper and it wasn't particularly bad sea weather, windy with gusts, and when the boat was seen last it had its sail up, her father was setting the fishing lines, a squall likely took the sail and capsized the boat in the blink of an eye. A wind that blows up only to drown six fishermen. They set fishing lines, each with his own thoughts and a shared anticipation of fish, the boat rises and falls calmly and then they're in the sea and none of them can swim, memories gather while they strike the water around them as if to grab hold of something, because although memories are precious they don't keep us afloat out on the sea, they don't save us from drowning. But which should the skipper try to save, his son or his son-in-law, or just himself? He hesitates, and in his hesitation he drowns.

Brynjólfur walks slowly along the dense streets of the old neighbourhood. Considers paying Gísli a surprise visit, had heard that the schoolmaster was having one of his drinking spells, but when Brynjólfur drew near Gísli's house he changed his mind and continued his rambling. Wanted to be alone and wade through the snow, difficult passage, Lúlli and Oddur hadn't begun to shovel here, always leave this neighbourhood for last, those who have less influence are frequently left for last. A dull light above the houses and around Brynjólfur, as if the air is a bit too thick or slightly dirty, and he thinks about his life.

Who understands existence?

Once everything was easier but now it has grown so terribly heavy and it's not as enjoyable to exist. Yet things were more difficult here before, he and Ólafía didn't have much money but had three children who were often sick, he sat there night after night with one or the other of them in his arms, listening anxiously to the child's unsteady breathing, and tried desperately to keep death away from their small, fragile bodies. It worked, somehow, they all lived, the two girls and the boy, Jason, who, to his father's sorrow, refused to go to sea. The one time Jason sailed was when he went along with his younger sister and her boyfriend to America ten years earlier, you should move here, they say in nearly every single bloody letter, it's much better here and it would certainly be good to let the sun shine on your old, tired bones. My bones aren't tired at all, Brynjólfur mumbles to himself, go, he says spitefully to Ólafía in his mind, it'll be good just to get rid of you! but bites his tongue at the same moment. Why isn't it enjoyable to look at her any more? Once it was life itself to wake up by her side, feel her thick body, rest his arm across her heavy breasts, then perhaps just hold her and say something, something out of the blue, and she would say something similar in return, it was so good.

So where did the joy go?

Bryndís, he whispers softly, tries to say this name out loud, as if to get his bearings, discover the taste. Oh, how delightful it would be to love again, then everything would be so bright. Bryndís. It's good to say this name, he lets it go and the air trembles slightly.

No, it's not possible to figure love out. We never get to the bottom of it. We live with someone and are happy, there are children, quiet evenings and many rather ordinary but good occurrences, on occasion little adventures, and we think: that's how life should be. Then we meet someone else, perhaps the only thing that happens is that she winks and says something perfectly normal, yet we are finished, completely hopeless, the heart pounds, it swells, everything falls away except this person, and several months or a few years later you've started living together, the old world has collapsed but a new one arises; sometimes one world needs to perish so that another can come into being.

Brynjólfur's smile fades a bit when he thinks about Ólafía. She looks at him sometimes with those large eyes of hers that remind him of the eyes of a sad horse, it would completely do her in if I got together with Bryndís. Brynjólfur has become sad again, continues his rambling, strolls around the old neighbourhood, sad about his life, at no longer taking any pleasure in touching Ólafía, it isn't because her heavy breasts have lost their ripeness, not because her body appears to have become greyer, no, this is something completely different, he simply doesn't know what it is and uncertainty is a destructive force. Sometimes he becomes out and out angry when the sad horse's eyes follow him around the little apartment, that's why he rushed out early this morning, drank his morning coffee so hurriedly that he scalded his tongue and still can feel it, muttered something about how he had things to take care of, had to hurry out before the anger burst to the surface with ugly and hurtful words, hurried out but could think of nothing else to do except hang around in Tryggvi's Shop, jabbering about worthless things, examining goods he had no interest in but still knew all about anyway, nothing to do but read a copy of *The Will of the People* that Gunnar loaned him. Read the paper carefully, although nothing captured his attention but an advertisement that read, *lost here on the streets a coin purse with 20 krónur in gold coin,* several silver and copper pennies and a gold ring, the finder requested please to return the purse to the print shop, for a fair reward. And Brynjólfur had thought, bloody hell, it would be good to find the purse, keep the money, then I could buy more than enough beer and whiskey without needing to write anything, but no, I'm incapable of that much dishonesty, I am such a great bloody weakling, and besides people would ask, where did you get this money? and what would the answer be? Brynjólfur walks in the snow along the narrow lanes of the old neighbourhood and is sad. Maybe he should put this announcement in the paper:

> Lost here on the streets of the town the purpose of life, the mercy of sleep, joy between me and my wife, my smile and eager anticipation. The finder is requested to return these to the print shop, for a fair reward.

Suddenly he's standing in front of Snorri's Shop.

Dammit.

It wasn't supposed to happen so quickly. There were still lanes left untrodden in the old neighbourhood, and he still had various things to contemplate. I should have gone to visit Gísli, then I'd be sitting there now, drunk and happy, thinks Brynjólfur, and he looks heavy-browed at the low-roofed, rather long house, Snorri's Shop, it says on the side, gold letters on a brown board, fading colours, fading life. The house lies lengthwise along Hansen Field and it's too late for Brynjólfur to turn round, the shop assistants soft notes of the organ coming from Snorri's apartment at the other end of the house. Snorri sits at the organ, music book open, joyful Mozart that was intended to enliven the morning, to nudge optimism or, rather, to haul it up from the depths, but the merchant managed only to play to the end of the first page and could go no further, not today, too far to Mozart, the ocean and half of Europe between them. So Snorri closed his eyes and let his fingers wander, they followed the sheet music in his breast and the darkness flows from the organ, penetrates the timber walls. This doesn't appear, however, to have much effect on father and son, they smile cheerfully at the captain, or up to him, they reach to just under his chin, he looks down at their pates. The son's hair is thin on the crown of his head but there's a prominent bald spot on the father's, who has worked in the shop from the start, both so faithful that uncertain wages don't trouble them, the son must be nearing thirty and still lives with his parents. Father and son often take a step back when someone comes in, instinctual courtesy. Torfhildur, the wife and mother, most often sits with them behind the counter, helping out when needed but otherwise doing some sort of handiwork, knitting a pullover, socks, mittens for her two men and Snorri as well. The three of them feel best together, Torfhildur, father and son, and don't need to say much to each other, are quiet because closeness says everything that needs to be said. Torfhildur always calls Brynjólfur her darling boy, although there's not much of an age difference between them, and greets him by stroking his cheek with her hard but warm palm, needs to stand on tiptoe to reach so high up. But now she's nowhere to be seen and unfortunately Brynjólfur is very relieved, yet feels ashamed because of it and asks, as if to calm himself, where are you little devils keeping Torfhildur, you can't be so wicked as to leave her behind at home?! Brynjólfur feigns cheerfulness, smiles broadly but feels a sting in his heart when it seems to him as if father and son darken suddenly, but then they both smile, she just doesn't feel well enough, replies the father, Björn or Bjarni.

The son: She had a really bad cough.

The father: She was sleeping badly.

The son: Or not well enough.

The father: No. And she had a fever.

The son: But it wasn't much.

The father: No, no, it's nothing.

The son: She'll be up and about tomorrow.

The father: Yes, it's nothing.

The son: No, nothing at all, not like that.

The father: No, nothing at all.

They stand close together, palms down on the counter, four trim, delicate hands side by side, and look at Brynjólfur with unexpected enthusiasm, as if they were trying to convince him and that it mattered that he agree with them. Thus they smile appreciatively when he mutters, no, of course it's nothing. On the other hand he feels like the worst traitor and says in his embarrassment, I'm going to start getting *The Hope* ready today. Yes, exactly, I just stopped by to let you know, can you please tell Snorri, I don't have time to chat with him now, the ship is calling, boys, and a captain must heed its call! He turns abruptly so as not to see the joy and gratitude that light up their faces, steps towards the door, the father comes running after him, wants to say something, but Brynjólfur doesn't give him the chance, opens the door and is already outside and putting distance between himself and the house, the father shouts his farewells and thanks after him; sharp little daggers that hit him in the back. Brynjólfur looks away before a house comes between them, father and son are standing in the doorway and start waving enthusiastically when they see his face, Brynjólfur's right arm jerks but does not go up, then the house blocks his view and instead of continuing in the same direction and heading down to Lowest Spit where *The Hope* lies up on the crest of the beach, he turns down the next lane and goes almost in the opposite direction.

XII

Geirþrúður is outside when the boy and Helga return burdened from the town, although it is mainly he who bears the load, uncertainty hanging over him like a shrieking tern, striking his head, he is covered in blood. Two ravens hop around ponderously a short distance from the woman, who scatters some food on the snow in front of the house, two others sit on the roof and wait, black shreds of the night. Helga stops in the middle of the street, likely so she won't frighten these black birds, the boy has never seen a raven come so close to a person, Geirþrúður could reach out and touch the one closest to her. She has swept the snow aside, created a large, empty spot and sprinkled something on it, it looks very much to the boy like pieces of meat, he glances at Helga, who appears completely unsurprised. The raven comes from Hell, one source says, flew black as coal out of the jaws of the Devil, who lent it his voice and his cunning. We sometimes call Geirþrúður Ravens' Mother. She started feeding the ravens shortly after her arrival here, it wasn't very popular but Guðjón let it pass, like everything else she got up to, the raven is a remarkable bird, he said when his friend Reverend Þorvaldur complained that Geirþrúður was attracting the ravens to the houses, and that it wasn't particularly cheering to wake up to their black croaking, you must appreciate that, Guðjón! Then Guðjón had looked out into the air and said thoughtfully, I read somewhere that in days of yore the raven made different, softer sounds, but that God has, for some reason, taken them from it and instead grafted to it a sound that was supposed to remind us of our sins, no doubt some damned nonsense, but nonsense can be entertaining, or what do you think, my friend? Þorvaldur said little, he was drinking at the time and had recently behaved very badly, wound up in Sodom and passed out there dead drunk, and thus had rather little interest in discussing sins and conscience and stopped talking about ravens, said nothing about how they often sat two-by-two on the roof ridge of the church when he pushed himself over there in the early morning, and had been doing so ever since Geirþrúður started feeding them. Ravens' Mother. It fit. Her hair was black like a raven's wing, her eyes dark pieces of coal that had lain for a thousand years deep down in the ground and had never been touched by light. The biggest gossips say she has a raven's croak for a heart, but you shouldn't believe everything people say. The ravens grab the pieces of meat, three of them fly up onto the roof to work on them, a fourth sits on the roof of Þorvaldur's house, croaks twice, perhaps startling someone inside.

Geirþrúður waits by the gate. She looks at the boy and he goes slightly weak at the knees, they come so close to her that he sees her dull freckles and immediately feels a debt of gratitude towards them, without them her face with its pitch-black eyes and high cheekbones would become cold and repellent. She extends her hand, he puts down the merchandise and her cold palm latches momentarily around his, hello, she says, and her voice is a tiny bit hoarse and dusky, he has just glanced briefly up at the ravens.

Then they are in the parlour.

Geirþrúður sits on a heavy green chair, he on a couch with large pillows and an incredibly soft cover that he strokes instinctively as he would a dog. He looks with great interest at an unusually large bureau with innumerable small drawers. Geirþrúður follows his eyes, do you like the bureau? It's big, he says, and has a lot of drawers. Yes, she says, it's necessary to get oneself a little coffer to which few have access, preferably none but oneself. The hoarseness in her voice isn't as noticeable indoors, her voice is softer and almost indolent, her black eyes rest on the boy, Ravens' Mother, these words shoot into his mind without him being able to do anything about it, he doesn't have much control over what shoots into his mind. Man is a peculiar creature. Has harnessed the powers of nature, conquered difficulties that seem unconquerable, he is lord of the Earth but has so little control over his thoughts and the depths beneath them, what dwells in this deep, how does it come into being, and whence does it come, does it bow down to any laws or does man travel through life with dangerous disorder within him? The boy tries to push everything unnecessary from his mind, a raven's croak for a heart, stories about Geirþrúður and foreign sea captains. She is wearing a white shirt and a long, black skirt, is it really called a skirt, he isn't sure, the black hair that lies across her shoulders and the green chair is either ruffled or ragged, as if she hasn't cared to comb it, she sits almost crosswise in the chair, arranges the pillows in the small of her back, dangles her feet over one of the arms, like a girl or an infant, yet is surely thirty-five years old. In contrast, the boy sits upright on this luxurious couch and feels ashamed of his stained woollen trousers. It is so miserable to feel ashamed of such things when one's friend has newly died, frozen to death right before one's eyes, when life appears not to have any purpose, no meaning, and one even plans to let the sea take oneself tonight, I'll likely be ridiculous until the very last moment, he thinks sadly. Geirþrúður strokes her lips with the ring finger of her right hand, very slowly, and then bites gently on the finger with white teeth, the incisor facing him is sharp, as in a predator. Helga comes in with coffee and cookies or cakes on a tray, it's difficult for him, having lived all of his moments in an ordinary home in the countryside and at a fishing station, to make a distinction between fine cookies and cake. The tray is probably made of silver, the cups white with a printed leaf pattern, oof, he thinks, while at the same time it's the only thing that comes to mind.

Oof.

Then his head is entirely empty.

Empty premises abandoned in haste.

He stares at nothing and the blood resounds in his ears like the escalating murmur of waves. Helga seems to be saying something. She is moving her lips, at least, and he asks, what? Geirþrúður looks at him, needs to turn her head nearly forty-five degrees in order to do so, her black hair falls like a wing across half her face, a trace of a smile is on her lips. I'm inside a novel! This thought strikes him and comes to his aid, saves him, somewhere he has read about all of this: a couch, chairs, such cups, these things called cookies or cakes and two women whom he doesn't understand. This is a novel, he thinks happily, and can even smile, I'm in a novel. The murmur of blood falls silent in his ears, he's inclined to lose his hearing, Helga is telling Geirþrúður, and his voice as well. I'm not sure I know how to drink from such fine cups, he then says apologetically, and adds, I've only come across them in novels, the latter statement intended as an explanation but of course it sounds completely absurd, they also look at each other, Helga takes a seat in a high-backed chair, she smiles, very faintly of course, but he is certain that this tiny change in her facial muscles is a smile and possibly in his favour.

You shouldn't let fine cups bother you, says Geirþrúður in her soft, indolent voice, but with a trace of hoarseness lurking underneath, the raven's croak on which she keeps a tight rein, the boy simply cannot control his thoughts, not one bit. It takes no special talent to drink from fine cups or eat with fine cutlery, although that might certainly be a widespread misunderstanding. Man is a creature, maybe a noble creature at his best, and he simply needs to eat, silver and porcelain don't change that fact, but silver frequently changes a man and seldom for the better, do you want to smoke, she adds, and is quickly holding a silver-coloured box, produces it by magic and pulls out a slender cigarette, the boy says, no thank you, but Helga accepts one, leans forward for Geirþrúður to light it, and the women both inhale smoke. Geirþrúður holds it inside for a long time, exhales slowly, then looks at the boy with her dark eyes, the smoke dissipates and vanishes, and she says, I'm very sorry how it went for Bárður, he was one of the few whom I really liked, you've lost a great deal. The boy takes such a large drink of hot coffee that he gets tears in his eyes, coughs twice, and the longing for Bárður nearly tears his chest apart, yet he says, like a complete idiot, this is very good coffee, and of course regrets having said it. Now it would be good if someone were to come in and shoot him in the head.

Geirþrúður waits until he has recovered himself after the cough, has managed without embarrassment to take another sip of coffee, then says, if you feel well enough to tell us, we would like to hear how it happened.

For some reason he isn't surprised at the request, and he doesn't withdraw into himself, on the contrary wants to tell about it, becomes perfectly enthusiastic, as if it mattered to sit there with these two women and tell them of the moment when he opened his eyes and saw Pétur's black head poking up from the floor, until he set off from the fishing station, to meet the night – to tell the story that lay from life to death. But he has only just begun to tell of how the trapdoor to the attic was raised and Pétur's head came up from the floor, like the Devil himself, and said, today we row, when someone knocks on the door, likely the one to the Café because the knocking is faint. The boy stops. The beer from Tryggvi, Helga says, stands up, runs her hands down her dress, looks quickly at the boy, wait with your story, and he nods his obedient head, listens to her footsteps grow distant. Tell me about yourself in the meantime, says Geirþrúður, almost without looking at him, he just barely catches a glimpse of her night-dark eyes as she turns her head to the side.

We never ask such things.

We only ask about things that are easy to answer and never let anyone near. One asks about fish, hay and sheep, not about life.

Geirþrúður sits before him like a poorly raised child, with night in her eyes, and asks him about what is innermost, and he begins, as if nothing were more natural, doesn't even say, well, there's not much to tell, which would perhaps have saved everything, showing respect to higher powers by displaying modesty, no, he says right out, my father drowned when I was six years old, starting in that way at the core itself.

My father drowned when I was six years old and then Mother was alone with us three, all young, my sister just a baby, we were quickly broken apart and each thrown in a different direction. I think this isn't a particularly good world we live in. I remember Father only hazily, and what I remember best I have from Mother, she wrote me a lot of letters and described him in them. Described him in such a lifelike way that it stuck in my memory and there hardly passes a day when I don't think about him and sometimes I feel as if he's watching over me, so I don't feel too much loneliness. His eyes follow me from the bottom of the sea.

He stops, almost frightened, almost angry at himself for having so unhesitatingly torn out his own heart and displayed it to an unfamiliar woman, there it lies in his outstretched hand, like a blind, whimpering kitten. The clinking of bottles and a distant sound of voices give him time to regain his composure. Geirþrúður no longer looks at him, she had turned her head to the side at the same time that he started to tell the story, stroked the raven's wing from her face, and now she looks over, the boy stares gloomily and full of self-contempt down at the floor, down into the soft cover which is reddish with an exotic flower pattern, everything is so alien now. Geirþrúður reaches for her half-smoked cigarette, he hears the quiet sound when she inhales, the embers glow stronger and burn up along the cigarette, life is glowing embers that heat the earth and make it inhabitable. You can tell me the rest later, she says when the silence has started to grow heavier around the boy and to oppress him. It was almost as if there were a trace of warmth in her voice, probably a figment of his imagination, he thinks, yet feels slightly better, or enough to look up and around him, regard the divided parlour better, even ventures to lean to one side so he can see better. The window in the outer parlour is considerably wider and larger, a huge, strong table beneath it and an extremely large chandelier above, he can see a corner of the piano, or what he thinks is a piano, and if he leans the other way he can see a large painting, no smaller than two metres square and displaying the whirling street life in a huge city, as if everything were in motion, the boy becomes a bit dizzy and straightens up again. He realizes that he has looked peculiar, leaning to one side, gaping like a stupid cow, but Geirþrúður acts as if nothing is out of the ordinary, she smokes her cigarette thoughtfully, he catches a movement out of the corner of his eye, someone is standing in the doorway. He looks around and sees Bárður's dead eyes in his white face and hears the precious voice of his friend in his head:

And there I was, thinking you were going to come to me.

XIII

His first job here in the Village, apart from going as a beast of burden down to the shop with Helga, was to open beer bottles for Brynjólfur and see to it that Kolbeinn had enough coffee in the large coffee pot Geirþrúður bought for him when she went to London two years ago. The pot cost a pretty penny since it had supposedly belonged to a famous poet, William Wordsworth, who composed many poems for the world, some of which still shine over tormented and arrogant humankind.

We mention this about the pot and its former owner because there are two things that matter to Captain Kolbeinn: poetry and the sea. Poetry is like the sea and the sea is dark and deep, but also blue and wondrously beautiful, there swim many fish and there live many kinds of creatures, not all good. We all understand Kolbeinn's interest in the sea very well, but some to be sure have difficulties understanding his interest in poetry. Naturally we read the Icelandic sagas, they have something to do with the nation and are sometimes exciting, quite boisterous and have heroes to whom you might possibly compare yourself, also natural to read a few folktales, tales of everyday life and deeds of derring-do, a poem here and a poem there, preferably by poets who write about their nation and know much about haymaking and the tending of livestock, but for a sea captain to value poetry as highly as fish, well, what kind of captain is that, in fact? And sure enough, Kolbeinn never found a wife and then he lost his sight. The light of day left him and the darkness settled over him. A vigorous seaman, nothing lacking there, tough as stone and could haul in the fish, certainly not much given to company and slightly sarcastic when speaking, but definitely not ugly and quite a promising catch, but never married and lived with his parents, then they with him when the years made them reliant on others. The dear couple. They were good people with scarcely a stain upon them. His father died first, at the time when Kolbeinn's fanatical interest in words and poetry had only just awakened, because of this the old man never got the chance to become irritated about the fact that his only child, his flesh and blood, wasted precious money on books. But his mother was smitten by this same interest and died underneath a German novel in Danish translation, lay reading in bed when death beset her, quickly but softly, and the book settled open upon her face. Kolbeinn thought she was just resting, this was at midday, she was old and rest is good for old bones, he kept as quiet as possible and didn't nudge her until two or three hours later, but there's little use in nudging the dead.

When Kolbeinn lost his sight he owned just under four hundred books. Some were large and expensive and came on ships from Copenhagen, like the book that killed Bárður. Naturally, a considerable amount of money went into his purchases, and the women who had dreamt of a life with this energetic but grumpy and sometimes peculiar sea captain thanked God it hadn't worked out, and thanked him even more when Kolbeinn lost his sight and thereby became a helpless wretch. We don't know when his vision began to fail, he hid it extraordinarily well, adjusted himself to the dwindling light, simplified his work habits, the crew naturally noticed the changes in his behaviour but blamed the man's waxing eccentricity and bookishness; as long as he continued to fish, it was his business. And that is what he did. Yet he had ceased long ago to discern his position against the mountains, it was simply as if he could smell the fish down in the sea. And then his sight extinguished completely. He went to bed and could still read by bringing his face almost completely up to the pages of the book, he could see his hands fairly well, saw the outlines of houses, but the stars in the sky were long since gone from him, and then he wakes in utter darkness.

First he lay extremely calmly and waited for his sight, or what was left of it, to return. He lay there as long as he could. Then started to move his head. Looked quickly from side to side, opened his eyes wide, rubbed them, but nothing changed, they were dead and the darkness pressed so tightly against him that he had trouble breathing. He sat up quickly to catch his breath, punched himself in the head, softly at first, then hard, hit it against the wall repeatedly and ever harder, perhaps in the hope that whatever had sprung apart would fall back into place, but the darkness stood firm, did not leave him. It had seized him and would never release its grip. Then he tottered out and made it safe and sound to his reading chair beneath the window, sat there upright, his face bloody, waited for his helmsman to arrive and thought a little about the knife that can easily cut an artery in two. But first he had to speak to his helmsman and then try to scratch something down on paper, however he could accomplish it. He owned more than a half share in the ship, all those books and the house, and it wouldn't do to die and leave it all without having settled it somewhere before that, otherwise rascals and sharks like Friðrik and Lárus would gather it all up and throw out whatever they didn't care about. Finally the helmsman came to check on Kolbeinn, who was always first to show up at the ship, but now the entire crew waited there scratching their heads, maybe you're sick, asked the helmsman hesitantly and felt a kind of coldness sift into himself, cold and fear, when he looked at Kolbeinn's face and saw the dried blood and the eyes horrifically empty. Kolbeinn turned his terrifying face in the direction of the voice and said calmly, decisively, you pilot the ship today, I am blind. Go. I'll speak to you later. And the helmsman drew back, scared of the blind eye, scared, as always, of that damned man, drew back and down to the ship, said little and revealed nothing until they were well out to sea, with five days of fishing ahead of them. Kolbeinn groped his way through the house in search of a pen and paper, fell twice over the furniture, in the second instance ran into the bookshelf, sat there a long time

Should I write that?

Of course not, don't be so bloody stupid.

Why do you think they'll appropriate what you own?

Because I'm a wretch and will soon be dead.

As far as I can … she stopped, continued, you appear to be living and breathing now. When he didn't answer she added, or so it looks to me.

Kolbeinn gave a little start but otherwise acted as if nothing was wrong and said, but you don't expect me to keep living like this, a blind wretch, useless to everyone, completely helpless and dependent?

Are you going to kill yourself, then?

What else should I do, dance perhaps?

You can live with me and Helga, we need company sometimes.

Are you calling me company?!

You'll get an excellent room that can hold all your books; you sell your house and I'll take over your share in the ship and we'll call it even.

When there is a choice between life and death, most choose life.

Geirþrúður took Kolbeinn with her through the Village and up to the house, like an old, wretched dog it would have been an act of charity to shoot. This was four years ago. Since then Kolbeinn hasn't gone any further than out to the garden gate, sits in the garden when the weather is mild and the sun heats the air, but otherwise feels best in the Café, gulping coffee, listening to the guests if any are present. Helga and Geirþrúður take turns reading to him, mostly in the afternoon or in the evenings when the darkness has softened the world and gone out into space after the stars, then they sit together in the parlour, this peculiar, profane trinity. We have never understood why she took the old sea-wolf under her wing, so temperamental and unsociable. They had known little of each other before, she had borrowed books from him on occasion, but perhaps they go excellently together; both of them blind, he physically, she morally.

But now the trinity is no longer a trinity because the boy has joined the group. He pours coffee into the mug that once belonged to an English poet, says, there you are every time, but Kolbeinn acts as if he's not there, as if he doesn't see me, mutters the boy to himself, getting a bit of a chuckle out of this.

He had told the trinity the story of how life changed to death.

Helga had returned and brought Kolbeinn with her and the boy told them about the sea voyage.

How Bárður had forgotten his waterproof, how they had rowed an unusually long way out. He told of how the weather had worsened, then turned cold, how a gale blew up, then how the waves started to dash over the boat. Bárður immediately became soaked and cold, so wet and so cold that it would have changed

194

nothing even if someone had loaned him his waterproof and thereby possibly sacrificed his own life, perhaps the lives of all of them. He who is soaked so far out on the open sea, in storm winds and frost, is doomed to die. The boy hadn't perhaps fully realized it then, or hadn't wanted to, and it's likely only now, for the first time, that it comes to him that the only hope was to get Bárður quickly enough to shore, to punch the ice and frost off the sail, off the boat itself, so it could attain a good speed. Yet that was still no hope, but instead more of a mirage. An illusion.

Then the boy told of how he went through the valley and the dark night with the book that killed his friend, nothing is sweet to me, without thee.

Geirþrúður listened with her eyes half shut, the white eyelids sunk over the night of the eyes; Helga looked at the red cover because eyes must be somewhere, they aren't like hands that can just sleep, feet that no-one notices for a long time, eyes are completely different, they only rest behind the eyelids, the curtain of dreams. Eyes must be treated with care. We must think about where we point them and when. Our whole life streams out of our eyes, and thus they can be cannons, music, birdsong, war cries. They can reveal us, they can save you, destroy you. I saw your eyes and my life changed. Her eyes frighten me. His eyes hypnotize me. Just look at me, then all will be good and perhaps I can sleep. Old stories, possibly as old as humanity, tell us that no living being can stand to look into the eyes of God because they contain the fountain of life and the abyss of death.

The boy described Bárður's eyes. Had to describe them, revive them, let them shine one more time. The brown eyes an obscure and foreign fisherman left behind on shore a very long time ago. Geirþrúður and Helga rarely looked at the boy as he told his story, Geirþrúður perhaps once, the other slightly more often, but the captain's blind eyes rested on him the entire time and didn't waver, cold, lifeless, darkened windows, nothing can come out, nothing can get in. The story went on longer than he had expected it to. He forgot himself. Lost himself. Left existence and vanished into the story, touched his dead friend there and revived him. Perhaps the purpose of the story was to resurrect Bárður, break into the kingdom of death armed with words. Words can have the might of giants and they can kill a god, they can save lives and destroy them.

Words are arrows, bullets, mythological birds that chase down gods, words are fish many thousands of years old that discover something horrible in the deep, they are nets vast enough to trap the world and the sky as well, but sometimes words are nothing, torn garments that the frost penetrates, a run-down battlement that death and misfortune step lightly over.

Yet words are the one thing this boy has. Apart from the letters from his mother, his coarse woollen trousers, woollen clothing, three thin books or pamphlets he brought with him from the hut, sea-boots and ragged shoes. Words are his most trusted companions and confidants but are still quite useless when put to the test – he is unable to revive Bárður and Bárður knew that the entire time.

This is why he stood in the doorway before and said, and there I was, thinking you were going to come to me, but left unsaid what the boy worked out for himself: because I cannot come to you.

There was silence after he finished his story, silence he himself broke by muttering, as if distracted, I need to write to Andrea and tell her I'm alive.

Silence after a long narrative indicates whether it has mattered or was told for nothing, indicates whether the narrative had entered and touched something or just shortened the hours and nothing more.

None of them moved until heavy blows unchained them. Someone was pounding on the house outside. Helga stood up, stood up slowly, then she came with a paper and pen that she handed to the boy and said, we should care for those who matter to us and who have goodness in them, and preferably never put it off, life is too short for that and sometimes ends suddenly, as you have come to know unnecessarily well. Then she went out to see what fist was responsible for the blows.

We should care for those who matter to us and who have goodness in them.

This must be one of the laws of life, and the Devil kicks the asses of those who don't heed it.

Helga's dress rustled when she left the parlour, she left behind a scent as well as the warmth that remained on the boy's cheeks after she stroked them quickly with four fingers. Old Kolbeinn stood up, murmured something softly and unintelligibly, used his cane to feel his way forward but carelessly, knew the way and crossed the room quickly, followed Helga, her fragrance and the rustling, and then the two of them were left sitting there, he and this woman with eyes as black as a January night. They looked straight at the boy as he held the pen, her inner life streamed from her eyes and was perhaps infected by their colour. We all liked Bárð ur very much, she said slowly, or, rather, softly and carefully, and will continue to miss him, each in our own way, which goes for Kolbeinn as well even though it looks like he's feeling almost anything other than regret. But you can easily count on one hand the people to whom Kolbeinn loans books, not to mention this book.

They heard Helga's footsteps approaching, quickly, calmly, some walk in such a way that it seems nothing can knock them off balance, as if they had no difficulty with any path, then there are others who are nothing but hesitation. So you see that footsteps can say much about a person: walk over to me, then perhaps I will know whether I love you.

It's Brynjólfur, said Helga in the doorway, and the boy thought he could see the faint smile on Geirþrúður's face, thirsty for beer, she added. You aren't happy about that, said Geirþrúður, still with her faint smile. Helga shook her head, he should already have started getting the ship ready, simple as that, she said. Nothing is simple, said Geirþrúður, but perhaps better that he's drinking here than with Marta and Ágúst. Geirþrúður acted as if she didn't hear Helga's snort, turned to the boy and said straight out, without

Words are inclined to jump like that out of him and therefore he often says things that are complete nonsense and get him into trouble or attract unnecessary attention to himself, which is almost the same as getting oneself into trouble. Sometimes he tries to make up for the nonsense by saying something immediately afterwards, but frequently only makes bad worse, and here he added, I'd actually got work in Leó's Shop this summer. Bárður and I made a deal with Jón, or, rather, Bárður did, it was he who got us the job, I got the job because of him and now he's dead and I don't know what's going to happen, he concluded this short, confused explanation, what the hell was I saying, he thought, and cursed himself. Geirþrúður did not let this bother her and simply said, he who doesn't know how to do anything has nothing to do in Leó's Shop, Tove would have you cut into bait after the first week and you'd hardly want that? But we here, the trinity, and now she clearly smiled, know better than Tove how to measure people like you. You know how to read and it's my understanding that you have good handwriting, isn't that right? The boy thought it enough to nod his head, didn't dare open his mouth and let some sort of nonsense slip out. Well, the little you know how to do is fine with us, there are precious few who know how to read in this town, because it's one thing to be able to read and another to know how to read, there's a huge gap between the two. I expect you'll be staying here with us, two weeks or twenty years, it's your choice, you can leave whenever you wish. You'll have the room you slept in and can try to make a deal with Kolbeinn about using his books, but wait a bit with that, let him get used to you, you'll read to him in the evenings and he'll soften up little by little. Otherwise there are several books here in the outer parlour, take the ones you want. There's just one other thing: you can expect to be sullied if you decide to live here with us; it's my fault, but you have to be able to take it.

I've always liked ravens, said the boy, again without thinking, the words simply rush out of him. Who sits down there and controls the words?

To his amazement and incredible relief they both smiled. He saw all of Geirþrúður's teeth, so white, two sharp canines but the front teeth in her lower gum were crooked, which is good, what is white and perfectly straight becomes wearisome after a time. Without sin there is no life.

XIV

And now he sits here. Over two sea captains and a dip pen. Which one should he write, *my dear Andrea* or *dearest Andrea*? Kolbeinn and Brynjólfur are sitting to his right at the corner of the table, Helga taught him what to do, to serve beer, coffee, how to record it, you call me if you can't handle it, then she was gone and he alone with the old men. Brynjólfur stares at him every now and then, his hair and beard ruffled, bring me a beer, you damned kitten, he calls in a thunderous voice although the first bottle is completely empty, he's like a calf with diarrhoea, explains Brynjólfur to Kolbeinn. But the boy couldn't care less about being called a damned kitten, a shitting calf, they're just words and are quite powerless if one doesn't pay them any heed, they just pass through and touch nothing. Besides, Brynjólfur has a greater and more intimate interest in beer than in him, and his temper grows softer the more he drinks. Two beers and the world is no longer wicked and full of all kinds of rubbish that irritates an honest man. Because we are honest men, you and I, he says to Kolbeinn, who says in his hoarse, almost grating voice that honesty is a luxury for spiritless angels, I don't understand you, says Brynjólfur, so deep-voiced that the fishes down in the sea tremble when he stands on deck and speaks loudly. I didn't think you would, rasps the other. Then explain it and may the Devil eat that puppy there, I think he's a spiritless wretch. Then the Devil isn't interested in him, says Kolbeinn, the spiritless grow angels' wings. You're strange, the giant rumbles, and that's why I've always liked you so much. Then the old seadogs start talking about fish and the sea and the boy stops listening, except with one ear and barely that, or just enough to notice when they ask for beer or coffee, it's safer for him to react promptly and efficiently, but when Brynjólfur has beer he can be alone with his thoughts, the other slurps coffee that is as black as the darkness surrounding him. They are of similar age but Kolbeinn's face appears to be older, by a difference of around a hundred years. They talk about the sea and about debauchery, they talk passionately about fish, cod swim in their veins, sharks dive deep down into their livers, there are storms and severe frosts and deathly dark seas, Brynjólfur sways and holds on tightly to the table so as not to be cast overboard, Kolbeinn's thick tongue licks the salt from his lips. The boy has brought eight beers to Brynjólfur, has poured coffee just as often into the mug of the English poet, the poet is thirsty, says Kolbeinn, and lifts the mug, the boy brings coffee at the same time, at first knows nothing about this Wordsworth and that he had owned the mug, flabbergasted that Kolbeinn should call himself a poet and becomes even more confused about him, what damned poet? asks Brynjólfur finally

Kolbeinn simply, and then they start talking about the sea again, they're immediately far out at sea, are in danger, the past frees them for a time from the present, from the depression, the anxiety, the darkness. The boy holds his pen but looks out of the corner of his eye at Kolbeinn, tries to figure him out but naturally can't do so, feels respect, a kind of fear, is apprehensive about having to read to him, to have to be near him, hopefully the women will listen as well, it would be better, will I read to him tonight? The sea-wolf, he then thinks, meaning the fish, is the sea-wolf always in a bad mood or is that just how it looks? He shakes his head, there's so little that he understands. He has written, *my dear Andrea*, and now adds, *I am alive, I made it all the way,* but then puts the pen down. Why in the hell should I live? I'm not interested in anything, least of all in this Ragnheiður, she's so cold it contracts my heart. I don't want anything and I don't desire anything. He stares confusedly at the pen. Absolutely doesn't want to die. The will to live sits in his bones, it runs in his blood, what are you, life? he asks silently but is so incredibly far from answering, which isn't strange, we don't have ready answers, yet have lived and also died, crossed the borders that no-one sees but are still the only one that matters. What are you, life? Perhaps the answer is found in the question, the wonder that is implicit in it. Does the light of life dwindle and turn to darkness as soon as we stop wondering, stop questioning and take life like every other commonplace thing?

The boy has started to think about the captain's library he has been imagining ever since Bárður told him about it, four hundred books, one probably needs nothing else in life, except of course sight, he thinks, even snidely, but is startled when the blind man brushes against him and goes into the house, shuts the door firmly behind him. Another beer, you wimp, says Brynjólfur loudly, and the boy brings him his ninth beer. The beer disappears into the giant, his body receives it endlessly, I'm so big, explains the giant to the boy, sit down here by me, dammit, or else I'll hit you, it's so difficult to sit alone, a man feels so lonely when he's by himself, you see, be good now and don't leave an old man.

The boy is good. He doesn't leave the table, can't get away for that matter, Brynjólfur has latched his large fist around his right arm. The boy sits next to the giant, who drinks beer, does so with gusto, then starts to tell about an old shipmate, Ole the Norwegian, they sailed together for a whole fifteen years, made it alive through wretched, ferocious storms and heaving seas, then Ole drowned in utter calm, his ship at the pier. Ole was piss-drunk and tumbled over onto his bald head, broke the mirror that was the Lagoon and disappeared, didn't even get to finish the bottle he'd bought from Tryggvi, French cognac that Ole had saved up a long time to buy. The body was dredged up and the bottle turned out to be half full and neatly tied to his waistband. Dammit, says Brynjólfur in the middle of his story about the Norwegian, closes his eyes halfway, holds his fingers in front of them, I can't see clearly any more! he half shouts in fear: I'm losing my sight, that goddamn bastard has infected me! I'm going blind! Brynjólfur closes his eyes but opens them again when the boy explains that after nine beers most people stop seeing clearly. The captain is so appreciative that he releases his grip on the boy, who rubs his sore arm under the table.

It is past noon and the sun would no doubt be shining through the Café's windows if it could make it to Earth through the clouds, yet it wouldn't have lifted itself high enough to shine on the Spit and the main part of the settlement surrounding Central Square, the Eyrarfjall peak rises into the sky and buries the houses in its shadow. But if there were a sun in the sky it would soon shine through the parlour windows of a house not far from the old neighbourhood, wherein sits a woman staring at nothing, she has big eyes, recalling a horse that has stood all of its life outside in heavy rain. She sits completely motionless, as only one does whom the joy of life has abandoned. Once, it was a long time ago, she laughed quite often and then her eyes were suns above life, the icicles that hung cold and hard from the houses turned into refreshing drops of water, where now is the joy in these eyes? The woman sits motionless, stares, a bit as if she were waiting for someone who has gone so far away that he might possibly not have enough time to make it back in this life. She sits bent over, her shoulders a bit hunched, she'll sit like this the whole day, and when it grows dark and everything becomes hazier, she'll resemble a mound more than a person. Where now is the justice in this existence, this wretched existence? You live with the most beautiful eyes in the world, they're as beautiful as the sea, then thirty years go by and they're no longer beautiful, they're just far too big and follow you around reproachfully and you see nothing but exhaustion and disappointment when you look into them.

Bloody hell, one looks into them and thinks of a rain-drenched horse, that's not to say a jade, are you nuts, boy, I would never call my wife by such a name and whoever says something like that will get to meet my fists! Brynjólfur hammers on the table, the boy jumps and the empty beer bottles Brynjólfur has lined up carefully in front of him clink loudly, eight, no, nine empty beer bottles. The captain grabs the boy's arm once more and unfortunately in precisely the same place, holds it tightly, there will be an ugly bruise there but the boy doesn't dare move. If only you'd seen my wife laugh before, huh, boy, and seen her eyes, oh, what has happened, where did the joy go and why did she need to change like that, where does this darkness and greyness come from? Do you know, boy, we played together with Kristján as children, we three were always together, no-one takes good, bright memories from a man, but bad memories don't disappear either, they grow more insistent over the years if anything, damn it all. Kristján drowned, did you know that, the sea took him, and that's of course the way we fishermen should go but I really miss him, I have so few people to talk to, you know that Bryndís is his daughter, Bryndís, that's a beautiful name, I'd imagine that God invented it so we'd feel a bit better. But, dear friend, I wish you'd seen her eyes before, not Bryndís but rather ... rather ... dammit, dammit to hottest Hell, I don't remember her name!

Brynjólfur sits there staring, perplexed, and doesn't remember the name that is ingrained in his life. The name of the girl he played with when youth shone over the three of them and they built ice-castles in the winter, played at being farmers together in the summer and sometimes she stuck buttercups in her hair and walked around just like the sun, she was the fairy tale itself. Brynjólfur wrinkles his brow, tries with all his might to remember her name and then automatically releases his grip on the boy's arm, and the boy sighs in relief but silently. Finally a gleam comes to his drunken and bloodshot eyes, like a glimmer before a clear thought, like a light deep within dim fog: I drink too much. He says this firmly and clearly, then nods his head in agreement with his own words and adds, yes, and then I betray everyone. Brynjólfur looks gloomily at the boy but seems to be having trouble seeing him clearly, leans his head back slightly, squints and repeats, everyone! I betray her, you know, my wife, and her eyes, I betray them every day. I betray Snorri and it hurts. I betray my darling boys, Björn and Bjarni, and I also betray Torfhildur. How is it possible to betray someone like Torfhildur, what sort of villainy is that? Think about it, this morning I wished she would die and do you know why? Because she is so good to me! She trusts me and speaks beautiful words to me but instead of being grateful I try to avoid her because she makes me remember the betrayal, imagine if she were to die today, or maybe tomorrow, wouldn't I just kill myself then? Still, I'm not evil, it's just this heaviness within me, here inside, he says, and strikes himself a mighty blow on the chest, there are some little black beings inside there and they've the boy's head. How long is your mother to wait, how long is your father to wait, and your sister, who is only three years old? Why should you live and not us? I don't know, mutters the boy, shivering with cold, then he straightens up in his seat, looks at Bárður and half shouts in his desperation, I don't know! Hush! Not a word! Brynjólfur thunders suddenly and grabs the boy's arm tightly, wait! Don't go! There's something happening, hush, not a word, it's coming! Brynjólfur leans forward, as if to listen, to catch a distant message, catch a name that life depends on his remembering, leans forward, shuts his eyes, his large head sinks slowly and he is asleep before his forehead reaches the tabletop. Then it's just the two of them, the boy and Bárður, he who lived and he who died. The boy pulls back his arm, does not look away from Bárður, who moves his cold-blue lips and says, I'm lonely here. I am too, the boy mutters, half apologetically, then he raises his voice and says, don't go, without knowing whether he means it. Bárður says nothing, just smiles bitterly. It has started snowing. The snow falls silently outside the windows, large, hovering snowflakes shaped like angels' wings. The boy sits motionless, angels' wings hover outside, he watches Bárður dissipate slowly and turn into chilling air.

Bárður reads from the Icelandic translation of Milton's *Paradise Lost* done by Reverend Jón Þorláksson (1744–1819), a prolific translator, poet and exponent of Enlightenment ideals in Iceland. To preserve the spirit of Bárður's reading of the poem in translation and to give a sense of how the text reads in Icelandic, I have re-translated Reverend Jón's lines into English, but here provide Milton's original lines for comparison:

page 27, "A cowl casts over all, accompanied by silence" – Milton: "Now came still Eevning on, and Twilight gray / Had in her sober Liverie all things clad; / Silence accompanied" (Book IV, 3286–8).

page 31, "And birds in nests for the night reposed" – Milton: "Now came still Eevning on, and Twilight gray / Had in her sober Liverie all things clad; / Silence accompanied, for Beast and Bird, / They to thir grassie Couch, these to thir Nests / Were slunk" (Book IV, 3286–9).

page 71, "of early-rising birds, a delight to the ears" – Milton: "Sweet is the breath of morn, her rising sweet, / With charm of earliest Birds; pleasant the Sun / When first on this delightful Land he spreads / His orient Beams, on herb, tree, fruit, and flour, / Glistring with dew; fragrant the fertil earth" (Book IV, 3330–4).

A GUIDE TO THE PRONUNCIATION OF ICELANDIC CONSONANTS, VOWELS AND VOWEL COMBINATIONS

ð, like the voiced *th* in *mother*

þ, like the unvoiced *th* in *thin*

æ, like the *i* in *time*

á, like the *ow* in *town*

é, like the *ye* in *yes*

í, like the *ee* in *green*

ó, like the *o* in *tote*

ö, like the *u* in *but*

ú, like the *oo* in *loon*

y, like the *ee* in *green*

ei and *ey*, like the *ay* in *fray*

au, no English equivalent; but a little like the *oay* sound in *sway* (*away*).Closer is the *œ* sound in the French *œil*